P9-CLS-668

COTSWOLD MANNERS

By the same author

FINAL ACT
PRIME MINISTER SPY

COTSWOLD MANNERS

An English
Countryside Mystery

by

MICHAEL SPICER

ST. MARTIN'S PRESS

ISBN 0-312-02562-9

First published in Great Britain by
Severn House Publishers Ltd.

First U.S. Edition

10 9 8 7 6 5 4 3 2 1

All the characters are totally fictitious and are not meant to bear resemblance to any living person

To my three children, Edward, Antonia and Annabel

CHAPTER ONE

I am thirty-five years old, five feet two inches in height. I have small boobs and fair hair, which I usually wear well down my neck. I have blue, almond-shaped eyes. Am I beautiful? Well, if beauty implies a certain grandeur, perhaps hautiness, the answer has to be 'no'; but I suppose I am pretty. I have to be honest, I am *very* pretty, especially when I have a slight tan. My prettiness must have a certain opaque quality which has so far been impossible to capture on canvas, though several artists have tried.

I was educated at Roedean and Girton College, Cambridge, where I read law with a view to becoming a solicitor like my father. But I married in my third year at university and so did not sit my Tripos exams. I was divorced four years later without having produced any children. I have never remarried, so I have kept the title. I am still Lady Hildreth. My former husband did remarry almost immediately, so there are two Lady Hildreths. I'm Jane; the other one's Elizabeth.

Lord John Hildreth was extremely rich, one of the richest men in the world, as a matter of fact. My settlement, which was made out of court, is certainly enough for me to live on. I have a very pretty stone cottage in the Cotswolds, a rather more elaborate establishment in Montpelier Square in London, and an apartment on 76th Street and Madison Avenue in

New York. My cash flow is sufficient to support these homes without worry. Even so, for the past ten years I have worked, rather hard as a matter of fact: for four as the public relations consultant of a well-known international cosmetics company, and for the last six for the Metropolitan Police. Actually, it's all a little more complicated than this, but more later of the precise nature of my present job and of how I came to change to it.

I merely mention all this at this stage not from any undue obsession with myself or my problems, but because I was directly involved, privately and professionally, in the strange, not to say frightening events I am about to relate. I thought it as well, therefore, to establish from the start who I am and what I do.

The story properly starts about eight years after my divorce. My former husband John was captaining his polo team at Cowdray Park in Sussex. Royalty were among the spectators and players.

I have never been very good at watching polo. As a matter of fact I'm not very good at watching any sport, with the possible exception of tennis. Sport is something I like to do myself. I am quite an athletic person (I was vice-captain of games at school). I can beat most amateurs of my own age at tennis and squash; I'm a fast swimmer and like to ride when I have the chance. But to return to the point, I don't like watching polo and, indeed, have never properly grasped its technical terms. However, I was not watching this particular game; I was in my apartment in New York.

The only reason for raising the subject at all is that in the third quarter (chukka, I think they call it) of the game in question, Antonio Alba, from Argentina, playing for my ex-husband's team, fell off his pony, broke his neck and died on the way to hospital. The autopsy showed that he had taken a heavy dose of drugs about an hour before the match.

The same night John, with whom I still maintained a relaxed relationship, telephoned me in New York to tell me of the disaster. Immediately after our divorce, Antonio and I had had a brief romance and my 'ex' thought I might want to come back for the funeral. It was very considerate of him, although I have to admit I hate funerals at the best of times, especially, I decided later, funerals of former lovers. Nevertheless, without hesitation, I decided to catch the next Concorde home.

I never did discover exactly why poor Antonio was buried in England rather than in his native Argentina. Perhaps it had something to do with the fact that he had spent most of his life in and around London; many of his close friends were English, although as he had been a world class polo player his acquaintances were pretty cosmopolitan. It has to be said also that he was not particularly choosy about whom he knew, as long as they were rich. In fact it was John Hildreth who made all the arrangements for the funeral – and this may itself explain why it took place in England.

A pretty elaborate affair it was too: Westminster Cathedral, Cardinal, the lot. As I arrived for the service I was shown by a swarthy, good-looking usher to a place near the front of the church. My companions in the pew were three rather attractive women. The two dark-haired ladies I knew quite well; the third, a redhead, I did not. All three blubbed on and off through most of the very long service.

I found the whole occasion distinctly gloomy and was determined to leave as quickly as possible when it was all over. Luckily I was sitting at the end of the row, so my escape did not look as if it would be too difficult. When Antonio's coffin had been carried down the aisle, I waited for what I considered to be a decent interval and while the rest of the congregation was still on its knees, set off in Antonio's wake.

As I reached the steps outside the Cathedral and was just about to head across the square to look for a taxi in Victoria Street, a hand grabbed my arm from behind me. I turned round to find John Hildreth standing alone at my side. He had aged considerably since I had last seen him, which must have been about six months previously. He had put on quite a bit of weight; his swept-back black hair was thinner; there was much more flesh under his chin; his face was rather pale. When I had been married to him his cheeks had always been rosy – perhaps, on reflection, more red than rosy. At that time I would have described his looks as rather boyish. Now, suddenly, he had become almost middle aged. He certainly looked every bit of his forty-two years.

I assumed that Antonio's death must have upset him. John and Antonio had played polo together on most of the great fields of the world. I have no doubt they shared women and probably more besides. They had been as close as two men of their type could be.

John kissed me rather formally on my cheek.

'I badly need to talk to you,' he said. His speech was slower, less crisp than I had remembered it. There was even a trace of a stutter in it. It was almost as if he had been drinking. I still felt a little jittery in his presence, and I recall on this occasion not wanting to look him straight in the eyes.

'What's the problem?' I asked.

He ignored the question for one of his own. 'Antonio. How well did you know him?'

'I think you know exactly what my relationship with him was.'

'I mean really *know* him.'

'How well does one ever really know anyone?' I said. 'I certainly knew him well enough not to want to continue our relationship.'

One of the reasons I had brought our not-very-long affair to an end was that I had not enjoyed the company of Antonio's gambling friends. (The other reason was that I had not enjoyed sharing him with several other women.)

'Anyway, he's dead now,' I added. 'So what does it matter?'

John stared at the ground; there was a silence between us, but it was not a comfortable stillness. John appeared nervous and I was beginning to feel uneasy myself. For a moment he seemed to have forgotten that I was there at all. Then he looked up. His eyes seemed to have become slightly bloodshot; perhaps they had been like that the whole time and I had not studied them carefully enough to notice.

'He deserved what was coming to him, Jane. He deserved it all.'

'Deserved to fall off his horse and break his neck?'

'He was up to his eyeballs in a lot of nonsense. Many of his mates were the scum of the earth.'

I wondered how deep the mateyness had really been. Antonio had not only played polo hard, he had also been an enthusiastic gambler, often playing with money that was not his own. This had undoubtedly earned him one or two serious enemies; it had not occurred to me before that John might have been one of them.

John seemed to sense that we were about to be disturbed. Grabbing my elbow, he edged me off the Cathedral steps and away from a small group of people that was building up to our left. His voice fell almost to a whisper.

'Look, Jane, I know this is all a bit awkward, you and I having been married and all that, but there really are things I need badly to talk over with you about Antonio. We can't do it here; there isn't time, for one thing. I need to talk to you professionally.'

'Professionally? What do you know about my profession, John?'

He hesitated; I thought he was about to answer my question directly, but just at that moment I noticed his wife Elizabeth approaching from behind him. He seemed to lose his train of thought. Whether he was disturbed by a shift in the focus of my eyes, I don't know. It was certainly the case that I began to take a close interest in his wife's arrival, and this may have distracted him. His voice began to contain an even greater urgency.

'I wonder whether you would consider coming down to Greysham Park this weekend?' For the first time in my life, he seemed to be pleading with me. 'Bring a man if you like. It wouldn't be difficult between us.'

I looked across his shoulder and could see the elegant shape of his wife drawing near.

'What would Elizabeth think of it?' I asked.

'Please don't be difficult, Jane. There'll be a small houseparty – about a dozen people.'

'A houseparty? Is this some kind of silly game, John?'

'All people who knew Antonio.'

I flinched. 'In that case, I'll know them, too.'

He nodded. 'I want you to know more about the company he kept.'

At that moment Elizabeth arrived and took up a stance at John's side.

There could be no way of describing Elizabeth except as 'beautiful'. 'Severe' perhaps, not my type at all, but certainly very beautiful. The most striking feature about her was her hair: rich, blonde highlighted and clearly worked into place with great care. It curved symmetrically towards her long elegant neck from beneath a wide-brimmed black hat. The latter she wore slanted forward to the left of her head. I can't recollect precisely, but I think the hat was made of felt, although it might have been mink to match her coat. In any event, it was a little too heavy for my taste. I would have preferred her in something more petite, possibly with a black net. She had clearly given a great deal of attention to her make-up. Her thin, unsmiling lips were painted with a sharp orange lipstick; her high cheekbones were accentuated with rouge – a little too deep, I thought – and the skin beneath her eyes was pasted with a white cream. Generally she had the appearance of having come straight from a beauty parlour, just having given herself enough time to wrap her long slim body into a fabulous black mink coat.

I hope all this doesn't sound in any way spiteful. If it does, I am sure it doesn't accurately reflect my view of Elizabeth at that time. Frankly, so far as one can ever properly assess one's own emotions, I don't think I had any passionate feelings for her one way or the other. My marriage was dead and I certainly wasn't jealous of her. The truth was I didn't know her. So far as I can remember, we had never addressed more than single word sentences to each other. 'Hello', 'Good-bye', had been about it.

On this particular occasion she ignored me completely as she said to John, 'Do let's go. I can't stand this a minute longer.'

As she opened her mouth, gold flashed between perfectly lined teeth. She spoke in a slightly clipped South African accent. Her voice, I thought, was pitched unnaturally high. She sounded a little hysterical.

John put his hand on my arm. I could feel its warmth through the sleeve of my coat, which I happen to remember was apple green and designed by Christian Dior. I had bought it at Harvey Nichols and was rather proud of its well-tailored line. John's touch made me suddenly feel protective towards him – sorry for him would perhaps be a better way of putting it.

'John's invited me to Greysham for the weekend, Elizabeth. Is that all right with you?'

Her blue eyes stared at me from beneath the brim of her hat. 'John's a big boy, and he does pretty well what he wants in our marriage,' she said.

Something at the back of my mind stopped me from giving her the reason for John's invitation. I had read a bit of gossip somewhere connecting Elizabeth in some way with Antonio. Probably untrue, but just as well to be careful.

'OK, John, I'll come, but I don't think I'll bring a man.'

The more I thought about it during the short taxi ride across Hyde Park Corner to Knightsbridge and Montpellier Square, the more I began to appreciate how out of character my former husband had been acting. John was many things: arrogant, amusing, bullying, even sometimes loving. But I had never before seen him furtive and suspicious and rather whiney.

CHAPTER TWO

Although I have only been back once, on professional matters, since the events I am about to describe, I still get a strange feeling in the pit of my stomach when I think of Greysham Park. I was, after all, hopelessly in love with John Hildreth when I first lived with him there. I sometimes ask myself even now whether I could ever love another man with such intensity again. The answer I usually come up with is 'no'. Of course, several other men have aroused me, in at least one other case passionately. I may even love someone again, perhaps even marry him; who knows, have children (though I've left that a little late now). But it takes the trust of youth to abandon yourself as I did to John.

Loving him at that time was an act of nature. I didn't try to rationalise it as I do now when I have a relationship with a man. I took the physical side of our love completely for granted. When we slept together in a strange room I didn't worry, as I do now, about the size of the bed or its position in the room. We just lay down together and made love, and went to sleep.

The whole thing was made easy for me, of course, by the fact that he was so damnably attractive. I have heard other women say that physical qualities in a man aren't important. Not as far as I was concerned. At that young age it mattered very much to me that

John should be so well-constructed. He was a good height – six feet two inches. He had a slim waist, which somehow supported the strongest torso I have ever seen.

When it was sweaty after polo his black hair fell in long strands down his forehead; otherwise, it was swept to the back of his oval head. When I was married to him he was a very funny man, though, thinking back on it, his jokes often had a cruel, personal twist to them. They were usually directed at lesser people than himself and of these there was, of course, no shortage. Whether you ranked him socially, physically, materially or intellectually, there was not much arguing the fact that John was superior to most other human beings.

One of his coarser friends once said to me, 'There are the rich and there are the f . . . ing rich. John is f . . . ing rich.'

I suppose I was fascinated at the time not so much by the wealth itself – very little of it ever came directly my way – as by the power it seemed to bring him. Someone once asked him whether he owned a ship and he had replied, 'No, I own fleets of ships.' He could have added that he possessed airlines, hotels in every major city in the world, and one of the largest chains of retail shops in Europe. He also owned Greysham Park, about which more later.

John's grandfather had been an arms manufacturer in Birmingham at the start of the century. Grandfather Hildreth had been given a peerage by Lloyd George for contributing to the war effort – at least that was the story the family told itself. John's father had taken the business forward into the Second World War. When peace finally came he had apparently launched a major programme of diversification, first moving into textile manufacturing and then into food retailing, transport and, just before his death on John's eighteenth birthday, into property.

John's mother had died of cancer ten years earlier, so naturally, as the eldest son he took over total command of the Hildreth empire immediately after his father's funeral. What's more, he was tremendously good at it.

Whilst still a teenager, he began rapidly to develop the property side of the business, somehow avoiding the exchange controls which were in existence at the time and which would have foiled lesser mortals. In the space of about ten years he managed to build one of the biggest property companies in the world. I married him when he was twenty-seven and, thinking about it now, at his peak.

His main source of amusement was polo. In winter he would shoot most weekends. He did this with the help of four beautiful black retrievers, Shirley and Bo, the two bitches, and Fred and Sam, the dogs. My favourite was Shirley, who was fatter and lazier than the rest and much more loving. She and I both found it rather a struggle working ourselves up to go out with the guns. Her misfortune was that it was her job to do so, whereas I know she would have much preferred to stay at home and have puppies. At Greysham she was not given the choice: like the others, she lived a rigorous regime in kennels up the drive, some way apart from the house.

Looking back on it all, I now feel that John probably married me in a fit of what I can only call lustful abandon. (I, incidentally, was just twenty, and the wedding took place in the family chapel at Greysham.)

From the start, it has to be said, there were certain irregularities about our marriage. We may have been passionate and relaxed when we were together; but the fact was that John was always away during the week. In a curious way this may have increased the awe and fascination in which, at first, I held him.

What I did find irksome even at the beginning was that I had no say whatsoever in the running of the house he left behind. I was, of course, more than content to have nothing to do with the estate; this anyway, to my innocent eyes, appeared to run itself, with the help admittedly of countless gardeners, gamekeepers and managers – all remote figures, shapes moving in the distance, camouflaged into the landscape. Occasionally I would pass one or other of them, carrying dead birds over his shoulder or supporting large baskets of cut flowers. There would be a 'Good day, yer Ladyship' and he would glide out of sight and beyond conversation through some wooden door or behind a bush. I was, in effect, totally untouched by what went on outside the house, except that I loved and admired its beauty. I certainly felt no responsibility for it, nor did I have any ambition to become more actively involved in running it.

It did irritate me, however, not to be allowed into the kitchen. While he was with us this was the undisputed domain of an Austrian chef called Fritz whom John had acquired from one of his better hotels. Rumour had it that Fritz had been an active Nazi during the war and this did not surprise me. Thankfully Fritz threw a fit of violent temper six months after I arrived at Greysham and left the next day after throwing a plate at one of the maids, narrowly missing her but smashing a Georgian decanter. His place was taken by Mrs Briely, much jollier but still totally possessive of her kitchen.

I wasn't even permitted to look after my own personal needs, like making my bed or doing my washing. This was all attended to by two housemaids called Sue and Amy. Sue had curly blonde hair, pretty blue eyes and was very well developed on top. Amy was rather the opposite: long brown hair with flashing eyes to match, and very slim. They were in a way perfectly balanced and I came rather to like them; this was probably because they were always so cheerful, even more so when John was around.

From my point of view the most significant feature of the domestic arrangements at Greysham Park was that all the staff took their orders direct from Leyland, the butler, and never from me. For his part, Leyland, who held the distinction of having served as the second Lord Hildreth's personal valet, always reported directly either to John himself or to John's personal secretary, Ms Carruthers. In the latter case it was always on the phone. On Ms Carruthers I pass no judgement as I never met her. I don't know whether she was married, divorced, or what used to be called a spinster. I have no idea whether she was pretty or ugly, old or young, intelligent or stupid. She must, I suppose, have been a good secretary because she remained a solid fixture at the end of the telephone for the entire period that I was part of the establishment.

Greysham Park itself is a large, rather complex, house set high in rolling Cotswold countryside, deep in the heart of Gloucestershire. The boundaries of the estate run almost up to the small town of Stow-in-the Wold. I suspect I would have rather enjoyed running affairs at Greysham. I think it is also fair to say that subsequent events suggest that I might have been quite good at it. But it was not to be.

John once told me reassuringly, 'Don't let it worry you. Just remember, it works by magic,' and the man with the wand was Leyland, good old trustworthy, all-powerful (under John) and definitely rather sinister, Leyland. I have no idea, incidentally, whether he had a Christian name. If so, it never came to my notice.

I must be careful at this stage not to sound bitter. To do so would be totally to distort the facts as they were. I was not bitter. Far from it; for a time I was very happy. Any – shall we call it 'objectivity'? – I have about the early days of my marriage I acquired gradually. Certainly at the beginning mine was the contentment of an unsophisticated and not very demanding young woman who was madly in love with her new husband. Even more to the point perhaps was that it was all so much more exciting than living at home in the outer fringes of suburbia, which my ageing middle-class parents called 'the country'.

At Greysham Park I was always busy if I wanted to be, when John was away. There was riding, fishing, eating (Fritz was a particularly superb cook; it was his one good quality) and boozing with married and unmarried girlfriends from neighbouring houses around the Cotswolds. On Tuesdays we used to arrange what I suppose was a sort of forerunner of aerobic classes, in the ballroom.

I became particularly friendly for a while with John's sister Louise. She was a year or two younger than I, and so was one member of the household who didn't overpower me. What is more, she had been brought up in Scotland by an aunt and was therefore almost as unfamiliar with Greysham as I was. I felt I could treat her as an equal. Although temperamentally we were quite different – she was black-haired and inclined to be fiery – we got along very well. She invariably arrived at weekends with car-loads of young people from London, always seemingly with a different boyfriend. It came as a bit of a shock when one day at the age of nineteen she suddenly announced her engagement to a Texan millionaire; it was even more surprising when she settled down apparently happily on a ranch outside Houston to bring up his family of three children by a former marriage.

Sometimes, initially to my relief, I found myself totally on my own. On these occasions I would spend a good deal of time in the library, a beautiful seventeenth-century room, whose ceiling was plastered in gold and blue moulding and whose walls were stacked with wonderful leather-bound books, most of which seemed barely to have been touched, certainly not by Hildreth hands.

I suppose one way of looking at this period of my life would be as having been wasteful, stifling, and possibly even rather humiliating. I didn't see it in this way at all at the time. For me it was the point in my existence at which I became free: if you like, when I became a woman. No longer the post-pubescent adolescent who had just shed her teeth braces, nor the student covered in headscarf and guilt about the need to swot for yet another exam, but a woman, a real lady. I don't mean the title. That didn't bother me at all. It still doesn't, though it meant an awful lot at the time to my parents. I simply revelled in the freedom of being able to decide for myself when to have a bath or to drive into Cirencester to shop, which pair of jeans to wear, when to go to bed, with or without my husband. I have, of course, learnt since that there is more to being a woman than to be free from your parents, but to begin with that was precisely what it meant.

After about three years – I can't put my finger on the precise moment – it all began gradually to fall apart. At first I started to resent John's long weekday absences, no longer being prepared to accept them as part of his exotic normality. Then I began to regret not having taken my Finals at Cambridge: on past form I would have got a first or at least a good second. It began to irritate me to think I would never know. Increasingly, as Friday approached, it was Louise's arrival with her young friends that I looked forward to, rather than to the familiar purr of John's Rolls Royce; and then Louise got married and Fridays became as dreary as any other day.

Nor would having children have helped. I wasn't ready for them – at least that is the way I felt about it at the time. What was perhaps stranger was that, as far as I can remember, John never once mentioned the subject. Perhaps he was just too busy to think about it much; perhaps he didn't want children by me. I don't know. But it was odd that a man with his wealth should not have thought more about an heir.

Our drift away from each other was, I now know, mutually felt, but there is no saying how long our marriage would have lasted had John not decided to take the initiative. If it had been left to me, it might have gone on forever. I am what is now called laid-back about my personal affairs, very much in contrast with the way I operate professionally. It's probably a mistake, but I am inclined to allow private matters to drift, especially when it comes to relationships with men; and that was certainly the way it was with my marriage.

And so it was left to John to do what I could have done just as easily and probably should have.

He chose a Sunday morning in early June. It was one of those days when the dew sparkled on the roses like crystals. The poppies in the herbaceous borders were opening into bloom. The croquet hoops had been set out on the west lawn, whose surface had been rolled to look like a vast billiard table. John had got up early, well before me, to exercise two of his ponies. He was halfway through his breakfast when I entered the dining room dressed in a pink dressing gown, which I remember had rather lovely white embroidery down the front. He poured me a glass of orange juice and for a while carried on reading the business pages of *The Sunday Times*.

Then, quite out of the blue, in a curiously matter-of-fact way, he announced that our marriage had become a bit of a bore. He was sure I would agree: these things were always mutually felt. He proposed in his words 'to go for a divorce' and to make sure I was generously provided for. I stared at him for a moment and then, with the arrogance of youth, said, 'OK, if you want it that way.'

I don't think he heard me. In his view he had already settled the matter. His statement had been one not of opinion, but of fact; it hadn't required a rejoinder from me. Thinking back on it, it was much kinder that he should have behaved in this way, rather than, for instance, engineering some long drawn-out quarrel in which I had my say, but where the break became messy and so more hurtful.

So far as money was concerned, John was completely true to his word. As I have already mentioned, I am not poor. In fact, I am rich, and for this I have John Hildreth to thank. My lawyers at the time advised me, rather unusually I have since found out, to grab the money, ask no questions, certainly make no difficulties, pay them a percentage of it, and run as far away as possible – or at least as far as the government of the day would allow me without taking most of it off me. (This turned out to be St Helier in Jersey). For these reasons the Hildreth divorce was the smoothest event of its kind imaginable. What's more, it was effected in almost total secrecy. The gossip columns made their revelations about two months after the whole thing had been signed, sealed and delivered.

And now, here I was, almost ten years to the day since I had been driven out of Greysham Park in the back of a Hildreth Rolls Royce, pulling the wheel of my own white BMW hard to the right and preparing to drive through the main lodge gates.

Ahead of me the tarmac drive wound downwards and to the left. As I drove into the estate I could just see, about half a mile ahead of me, poking up from behind a gently sloping green hill, the tops of the tall Cotswold stone chimneys of the big house.

The sight which held for me so many good

memories somehow managed now to fill me with a sense of foreboding. I remembered again the puzzling look in John's eyes as we stood on the steps outside Westminster Cathedral. Whether it was some premonition, I do not know, but suddenly I began to regret having accepted his invitation. As I drove along the drive I even began to look out for the side roads, half toying with the idea of turning round and going home.

I must, of course, be careful as ever not to exaggerate; not to allow my memory to race ahead of events; not to attribute to myself emotions which I would have felt had I known what lay ahead that weekend. Had I been able to anticipate what was to take place, I might well have been very frightened. This itself would not necessarily have deterred me from driving on; as will perhaps become apparent, I am not by nature cowardly; one might even argue that it would be better sometimes if I were a little more nervous about my physical safety. This was certainly one of those occasions when it would have been to my great advantage to have been a little more cautious, a little more sensitive to potential danger. As it was, my mood can best be described as gloomy, but I did not turn back.

CHAPTER THREE

Greysham Park was built in the reign of King James the First. I think I read somewhere that the first stone was actually laid when the old Queen was still alive. Certainly much of the architecture was recognisably Elizabethan as opposed to Jacobean. The main entrance in particular, with its gently rounded top, was definitely in the Tudor style.

The house had originally been built in the shape of a T and this still formed the main part of the building. The cross-bar of the T made up most of the public rooms. These were the South Rooms, the Hall, the Red Room, the Drawing Room, the Dining Room and the Library. Each of these looked out west across the main lawns for five miles down one slope and up to the crest of another. On this far hill there seemed on winter days to be a permanent silhouette of riders from one of the Cotswold hunts projected against a watery sky.

At the northern end of the house the first Lord Hildreth had built a ballroom which one reached through a panelled passage that ran along the entire length of the north-south section of the building. The ballroom jutted out westwards, so forming a pretty courtyard walled on three sides; the centrepiece of this courtyard was a stone pool and fountain.

The leg of the T comprised the kitchens, gun and

saddle rooms. Above these, on the first floor, were ranged most of the ten guest rooms, each with its own bathroom and dressing room. To the east of the base of the T, two or three hundred yards away from the house itself, lay the family chapel, in which forty people could sit in great discomfort.

Such was the structure of the main buildings of my former home, which I now approached one afternoon in late summer. On this occasion they had a slightly sinister quality, the explanation for which I could not for the moment put my finger on, but which had definitely not been apparent to me when I lived there.

As I parked my car close to the main entrance, I knew at once that I was not the first guest to arrive. Neither the red Porsche nor the green E-type Jaguar standing alongside my BMW were likely to belong to John; they simply were not his style – too flash, not formal enough for him. I guessed that they hadn't been there long enough for one of the grooms to have driven them away to the garage.

I looked across my shoulder to my left and was not entirely surprised to see a helicopter parked on one of the south lawns, almost hidden by a bed of large shrubs. It could only belong to John's younger and only brother Michael.

Michael was very different from John, in his taste for travel as in many other ways. To begin with, Michael was a skilled helicopter pilot, having been trained to fly by the Royal Navy. He was also, incidentally, an international skier, a one-time scholar in mathematics at Cambridge University, a serious bridge player, winner of two fortunes and loser of one. To cap it all, he was one of the best-looking men I have ever met. Well over six feet tall, with long flowing fair hair, he had a perfectly chiselled square face, into which was set a pair of voluptuous lips and straight white teeth to match. Whereas John had a body which was thick and sturdy, Michael's was athletic and wiry. The only physical characteristics the two brothers had in common were a pair of mocking blue eyes, which, to my knowledge, both used to good effect on the opposite sex.

Since my divorce from John I had made a habit of steering as far away from Michael Hildreth as I possibly could. The reason quite simply was that I didn't trust myself with him. My feelings about Michael were actually rather complicated. On the one hand, I confess I found him physically very attractive. I also admit the more often I had bumped into him at Annabel's, Ascot, or wherever, the more the attraction had grown. On the other hand, I knew him to be a ruthless cad, especially where women were concerned. I was to learn much more about Michael and his habits in the days to follow.

The only thing that was clear to me as I turned off the ignition and opened my car door was that the presence of the familiar helicopter meant that Michael Hildreth was to be one of the house party gathered at Greysham for the weekend.

I had given some thought to what I should wear for my return to Greysham. I am not sure whether in the end I got it quite right. Looking back on it I think I arrived rather overdressed. I had chosen a suit with a three-quarter length green cotton skirt, tight fitting and with a matching jacket. The latter, I remember, had puffed-up shoulders made fashionable at the time by the Princess of Wales and by one of her favourite designers, Bruce Oldfield. I remember also having to struggle a bit to get out of the car and being grateful for the slit at the back of my skirt. Without this it would have been practically impossible to swing my legs onto the drive with any dignity.

The only reason for being bothered at all about what

I looked like as I emerged from the car was that my arrival coincided exactly with that of the butler, Leyland. At the precise moment the engine of my car was switched off, the studded oak door swung open and the ageing (and, I thought, leering – but that might have been my imagination) Leyland stepped into the drive and presented himself before me.

As was usual during the period of the day when guests were expected to arrive at Greysham, Leyland was dressed in his morning suit outfit: somewhere between a butler's uniform and a wedding suit, comprising a short black coat and grey pinstripe trousers. His routine for greeting had not changed much either since I had last witnessed it: a shake of the hand, an implausible word of welcome. This was usually followed by an act of swift disappearance. It was left to lesser men and women to cope with such practical details as the carriage of bags from the car to the rooms, the garaging of the cars, and the drying of wet clothes.

Over the years, Leyland had cultivated and, indeed, refined many of John Hildreth's mannerisms. I noticed that he now had a fully developed version of the mocking smile and a passable approach to the smoothing down of the hair (in his case now white) with the flat of his hand. There was even the foot-scraping motion when on the defensive. But, again, I must not exaggerate: Leyland had his own personality, cold and polite and pseudo-deferential.

He stood before me, about five feet ten in height, with his feet together and his head held slightly askew to the left as if he had a minor deformity of the neck. He had allowed his hair to grow longer than when we had last met, although it was now thinner and whiter and swept back, whereas before it had been parted to the right. His features had become more exaggerated. His small oval face was more lined, his nose more pointed, and his eyes, which were blue, more slit.

Leyland was not an ugly man. As a matter of fact, I can imagine a certain type of woman, someone who liked public obsequiousness combined with private tyranny, might go for him in a big way.

'Welcome back, your Ladyship. It's been such a long time,' he intoned.

'I see Mr Michael is down for the weekend,' I said with as credible an appearance of disinterest as I could manage. Leyland raised his eyebrows uninformatively, very much after the style of John Hildreth. I smoothed down the back of my skirt, which I sensed had creased during the half hour drive across the Cotswold hills from my cottage at Chipping Campden.

This was the point at which in the old days Leyland had typically done what John used to describe as 'a bunk'. On this occasion he lingered beside me. For a moment I thought with some distaste that he was about to honour me with some great confidence or perhaps, a little more acceptable, with a new piece of scandal. (He had always been a gossip: it was one of his more attractive characteristics.) Neither was to be: he simply wanted to have a bit of a grumble.

'We're almost a full house for the whole weekend, my Lady.' He shook his head sadly. 'We don't have the type of staff we used to have, either.'

Poor old Leyland. I wondered whether this meant I was going to have to carry my own bags. It was quite clear that he had no intention of doing so.

'The weather forecast is uncertain,' he droned on. 'I can't imagine what his Lordship plans to do with everyone in the circumstances.' Then he seemed to brighten up. 'Knowing his Lordship, I suppose we can be confident that if anyone can think of ways to amuse them, he will.' He gave a grin, the like of which I had not seen before. The ends of his mouth moved a few centimetres sideways while his lips remained tightly pursed together.

I decided I had had enough of this and changed the subject. 'Where is his Lordship?'

'In the gunroom, my Lady.' I thought I detected a new sulkiness in his voice. I decided to push my luck. The man seemed to be on the defensive.

'And Mr Michael?'

He looked at me in a way which I thought showed some distrust, even suspicion, and said, 'With his Lordship in the gunroom.' He paused and then seemed to relent. 'He arrived about an hour ago. They've been together ever since. His Lordship is worried about a pair of Churchills he bought last week from Carey's in Ledbury.'

'They wouldn't sell him anything but the best.'

This remark seemed to realease an uncharacteristic flood of warm emotion deep inside the Leyland breast.

'No doubt he wants a second opinion from Mr Michael. My own view is that they are beautiful guns. I have told his Lordship he should stick to his first impressions. In his case they are usually right.'

We were still standing outside the front door in the middle of the drive and I was beginning to feel a bit awkward.

'Now that we've exhausted the topic of his Lordship's new guns, perhaps I might ask when shall we get to see the great man himself?' As soon as I had posed the question I regretted that its slight touch of sarcasm might have given an impression of intimacy. There was no way I wanted Leyland of all people to feel that he had been taken into my confidences.

Thankfully, he didn't seem to have noticed the irony. 'His Lordship said he would meet everyone for drinks in the drawing room at seven-thirty.'

'Did he just? I was becoming distinctly irritated. I looked at my watch. 'That's in three hours' time. I could have stopped to do some shopping in Burford.'

Leyland gave a slight nod, which I took as some sort of gesture of apology.

'Well, it looks as though it's her Ladyship for me for the rest of the afternoon,' I said. As a matter of fact, the idea of a session alone with Elizabeth quite appealed to me. Probing at her beautiful steely armour would be a challenge of sorts. I wondered for a moment whether I could make her cry; perhaps that would be easier than to make her laugh. I imagined that Elizabeth had never really laughed. Not from her belly, doubling up and making a loud noise; it seemed pretty improbable – as improbable as that she had ever torn one of her elegant dresses or forgotten to put her make-up on when she went shopping. For that matter, she would be a little out of place in a shop.

'Her Ladyship?' Leyland seemed puzzled.

'The other Lady Hildreth. My successor, the one who took over from me. My hostess for the weekend.' I allowed my irritation to carry me away a bit.

'Oh, she's not here, my Lady.'

'Not here?' This was an unexpected development. 'Does she plan to be away for the whole weekend?'

'We're not sure, your Ladyship. She comes and goes . . . how shall I put it? Erratically.'

'Does she just? What does his Lordship make of that?'

Leyland passed his hand through his hair and changed the subject, in the professional manner for which he was so respected throughout the county and, no doubt, much farther afield. 'Some of the guests are already having tea in the South Room. Might I suggest you join them there, my Lady? I will arrange for your bags to be taken up to your room. I believe you are in number nine, overlooking the rose garden. As I recollect, it was one of your favourites amongst the guestrooms.'

I do not remember ever having expressed a preference for any of the guestrooms, certainly not to Leyland. My suite, or rather, *our* suite, had been on the south-west corner of the house.

I had no intention, however, of arguing the point with Leyland. Neither, on the other hand, did I wish to leave him with the sense of having done me a favour. The last thing I wanted was to be in any sort of debt to the man. So, in a tone which I contrived to make as offhand as possible, I said, 'I don't seem to have much choice, do I, Leyland? But that's fine. If you arrange for my bags to be sorted out, I'll go along and meet the others. Oh, and by the way, I'll unpack everything myself. I really mean that – I'll do my own unpacking.'

I was determined to rub the last point home. The prospect of my evening dresses remaining crumpled for another hour was definitely to be preferred to a member of Leyland's army, depleted as it might be, rummaging through my suitcase. It was not, on this occasion, a matter of security: there were no weapons in my luggage. It was simply a question of privacy. I may be a little bohemian in some ways, a bit vague in my private life, but I didn't, and I don't, like strange hands fingering my personal belongings. I am still amazed, when I am involved with airport work, how few women complain when their handbags are intimately searched by seedy fat little men dressed in neo-Gestapo uniforms. In any case, on this occasion, if there were crinkles in my clothes (the long, green silk evening dress was particularly vulnerable) they could be ironed out while I was having a bath. As it turned out the number of creases in my dresses was not to be my main concern over the next few days. To put it mildly, there were other distractions which effectively took my mind off the state of my wardrobe.

CHAPTER FOUR

I re-entered my old home for the first time in eight years through the Tudor front door and with some foreboding. To this day I cannot fully explain the reason for the unease I felt.

Perhaps it was just that I wasn't particularly looking forward to John's promised analysis of the life and times of Antonio Alba. I especially didn't want to have to go through the process of getting to know any of his friends again. I had enjoyed Antonio for a while when he was living, but had no great wish to pore over his entrails now that he was dead. Perhaps I was unconvinced that Antonio's death would have much to do with why I had been invited back to Greysham. Elizabeth's absence certainly suggested another possible explanation.

John would no doubt have heard of some of my professional – perhaps even my private – exploits. Possibly these had reawakened in him an interest in me; perhaps he was planning to work this up into a full-blown affair.

Somehow, though, this did not quite ring true either. It wasn't John's way of doing things; or at least it hadn't been in the past. When I had last known him well, he would have been far too proud, too detached, to have resorted to a squalid little trick of using Antonio's death as some sort of pretext for asking me down for a dirty weekend while his missus was away.

I certainly very much hoped this was still the case; I had absolutely no desire to revive the past with him. Any feelings I had had for him were over, or so I thought. I had sensed some sympathy for him on the steps outside Westminster Cathedral; he had seemed strangely vulnerable when I had met him on that occasion, but there had been no physical arousal, none at all.

I have to admit the whole subject of my relationship with John worried me quite a lot. It would have been very unfortunate if I had found myself having to fight him off in some way. The last thing I wanted was to make an enemy of him. Given the extent of my spending habits and of his support for them, that would have been very silly. No, I very much hoped that there wouldn't be any kind of a scene with John Hildreth; he was far too important to me. I hoped there wouldn't be any kind of a scene with his brother Michael, for rather different and less logical reasons.

I think it was the shock of the darkness inside the front hall which for a moment put all these thoughts out of my mind. After the sunlight outside I found it hard to adjust my eyes to the unlit interior. I remembered that Leyland had said that the others were in the South Room. Instinctively I turned to my left and felt for the round gold-plated handle of the door in front of me.

In view of what took place later, it is of some importance that I now describe with care the scene which met me as I opened the door of the South Room.

As its name suggests, this was located at the very southern end of the house. Its gabled windows looked out across lawns both to the south and to the west. On a fine day the South Room was filled with sunlight from lunchtime to dusk; this was one reason why it was so heavily used in the afternoon. Another was that it was the only really cosy place in the entire house. It was the one room at Greysham in which you could sensibly curl up on the floor and fall asleep in front of the fire. It was the one room also which John's mother had not attempted to redecorate. When I had lived there it had always pleased me that not one of the seemingly endless stream of interior designers who had spent weekends at Greysham had persuaded John to permit them to 'have a go at the South Room'. Frankly, Greysham needed the tattiness of the South Room as a relief from the perfect post-war formality of the decorations of the rest of the house.

When I entered the room it was pretty well in the same state as when I had left it. The faded orange wallpaper was peeling a little further down from the ceiling. The seats on the gilt sofas sagged closer to the floor. The gash on the leather armchair had widened and, something new, woollen effervescence was blowing from a cut in the seat on the fireguard. But nothing fundamental had been altered. It was the same old South Room, inviting and pleasing.

Not so welcoming were the people in the room. As I came in, everyone stopped talking. There was complete silence: not a polite inquiring silence, but a sullen, even resentful, possibly fearful, hush. No, that may be going too far, again wrongly attaching in retrospect a mood appropriate to events which had not yet taken place. There was no way that I could have sensed at that moment that they were fearful. I distinctly recollect, however, that they sat completely still as if in a photograph. It must have only been for a few seconds, but the scene made a vivid impression on me. I can still recall it precisely.

Lucy, Michael's wife, was sitting on the fireguard. Her white face peered at me from behind strands of long, brown hair. Her blue eyes were vacant. I wondered what brand of drugs she was into this time and hoped she wouldn't tell me. It could cause me professional embarrassment.

Bobby Longfellow sat upright on a sofa. The late afternoon sunlight was reflected on his bald head. His short legs were crossed at the ankles. I suspected he was too fat to cross them higher up. Bobby was Member of Parliament for somewhere in the Midlands, very rich and a patron of the arts. The Longfellow money had been passed from father to eldest son since the Middle Ages. It was rumoured that Bobby was married, though his wife, if she existed, was never in attendance. His interest in women was oblique. I was not alone in suspecting him of the most horrendous perversions. Bobby worried a great deal about his health and had an obsessive fear of death. For this reason he varied his periods of heavy indulgence in rich food and booze (he was particularly fond of American cocktails, with a special emphasis on White Ladies) with bouts of total abstemiousness, when he drank only still Malvern water and ate Ryvita biscuits.

His political life was, like the rest of him, unusual. I'm told he was capable of the most brilliant speeches, though, characteristically, these were rarely topical and therefore did not hit the headlines. He attended debates infrequently, preferring (when he was not being abstemious) to sleep off his lunch in the House of Commons Library before returning to his flat to prepare himself for dinner. Gossip had it that his relationship with his constituency was surprisingly good. If true, this was probably because he had a large house in its centre from which he dispensed generous and carefully constructed hospitality. When he was at home, Sundays were 'open house' when as many of his constituents as could sit themselves around his kitchen table (I gather it could take about twenty at a time) would fill themselves with exotic food, which he usually cooked for them himself.

Although he did not play polo (I doubt if he engaged in any sport), Bobby bred polo ponies at a stud on the grounds of his country home. He also organised matches, in which Antonio had been a frequent participant. Indeed, Antonio and Bobby had a relationship (friendship would have been the wrong word – Bobby didn't make friends), a relationship which went deeper than polo. I was never quite clear as to its exact nature although it was manifestly not a physical one; but I was certain at the time I knew Antonio that whatever he had going with Bobby was a major source of the funds which enabled the Argentinian to maintain his brilliant performance on the polo fields of the world.

Stretched out on a sofa opposite Bobby Longfellow was a man of very different character. About ten years younger than Bobby and in his late thirties, Giles Lester was tall, lean, unmarried and very athletic. He also knew how to make money fast, and having lost it, how to make it again. First generation public school, his jaunty arrogance hid a lack of confidence which women generally seemed to discover after, but apparently not before, they had been to bed with him. When Giles and I bantered with each other, as we had from time to time, we masked a genuine dislike for each other. I know he deeply resented the fact that I was one of the few women (perhaps the only one) on whom he had set his sights who had not succumbed to his charms. It irritated him even more to know that this was not because I was frigid or totally unattuned to the ways of the world.

Some years previously Giles had physically assaulted Antonio when the Argentinian and I were dining alone together in a restaurant in Chelsea. Giles must have followed us to the place and the attack must have been planned. Whatever the circumstances,

Giles had to be driven to hospital with a broken jaw. His psychological recovery was slower than his physical, although he wasn't able to eat properly for several months.

I am sure now that part of his dislike of me was a reflection of his growing hatred for Antonio. This seemed to develop into an obsession when Antonio began not only to excel against Giles on the polo field but to build a more extravagant lifestyle than the one Giles for a period had been able to maintain for himself. The purchase by the Argentinian, after one of his visits to Bobby Longfellow, of a twelve-berth cruiser which he moored at Cannes seems, on looking back on it all, to have been something of a watershed. After this, Giles and Antonio, so far as I am aware, never spoke to each other again.

All this would have been simply childish had not there been more sinister undertones to it. Giles Lester was something more than a clever spoilt brat, though he was all of that. There was about him a touch of embryonic lunacy which went beyond the bounds of the tantrum and the unpredictable response. You never quite knew how far he would go in pursuit of his emotions.

Sitting on the same sofa as Giles, holding his feet on her lap, was Sylvia Richards. Giles had kicked off the Chinese slippers he had been wearing and Sylvia was massaging his toes through his socks.

At the time of Antonio's death Sylvia had been sharing him with Annabel Silvester, who now sat in a window seat beside Robert Luke. It was said that Sylvia and Antonio had sex in common, whilst Annabel and Antonio shared an interest in horses. Each had enjoyed the benefits of his growing fortune. Over the past year or so, the three of them had lived together in a house in Wellington Square off the King's Road in Chelsea. 'Lived in' is perhaps too inexact.

Wellington Square was the base from which they moved out to Cannes, Buenos Aires, New York and, above all, the Longfellow mansion in Warwickshire.

Sylvia was fair and slim and whiney. Annabel was buxom, deep voiced, dark, intelligent and good with horses. She disliked Giles Lester almost as much as I did, partly, it was thought, because she was one of the few women he had not made a pass at, but also because she considered him stupid.

Antonio seemed genuinely to have found fullfilment in these two women and they increasingly began to see themselves as his two wives; the feeling was apparently mutual, so much so that he was said to have included them in his will.

Lastly in the South Room that afternoon there was Richard Luke: wiry, quiet, distantly related to the Royal Family, but above all, the son of an investment banking tycoon from whose empire he drew money but not employment. Richard's primary interest in life was to gamble. He was a good sportsman and a regular polo player, but it was at the backgammon table that he first came to know Antonio, and it was through gambling together at tables around the world that Richard and Antonio became for a time the nearest thing to firm friends that it was possible for two such men to be. This very close acquaintanceship led Richard inexorably into the sphere of Bobby Longfellow, whose contemporary he was.

Bobby's influence over Richard grew in leaps and bounds when Richard lost his part of the family fortune and was subsequently disowned by his father. As Richard came increasingly under Longfellow's powers, so the nature of his relationship with Antonio seems to have changed from that of comrade to that of servant, or at least employee. I had been with Antonio on at least two occasions when Richard had been kept waiting in another room for what amounted to an audience, in a way which would have been unthinkable a few years earlier.

I felt a certain sympathy towards Richard. He was the nicest person in the room, the competition, admittedly being pretty weak.

I'm sure I was the first to speak. I said something banal like 'Hi, everyone,' and as if they had been drilled to it, they responded in a sort of chorus. 'Jane? Hello.'

Then there were variations at differing levels of descant: 'What a surprise.' 'You're the last person I expected to find here.' 'My God, you're as beautiful as ever.' 'Where the hell have you blown in from this time?' 'Can't fathom it out. Wish I knew what you do with yourself these days. Never around like you used to be.' Then silence again. I went to the mahogany round table in the centre of the room and poured myself a cup of tea from a silver pot. It was a good spot from which to survey the crowd.

I have taken some time to describe my fellow guests in the South Room. What happened next, however, took place while I was still pouring out my tea and before I had had time properly to reconsider the significance of Elizabeth Hildreth's absence. I wondered for a moment whether this was some sort of confirmation of the recent rumours I had heard that all was not well between her and John.

As I put the teapot down, Giles Lester pushed Sylvia Richards away with his left foot and almost shouted, 'Why couldn't Lord bloody John Hildreth have told us that that woman was coming?' I think he pointed at me but that is a matter of detail which I may have misremembered. He was certainly referring to me.

'Because if he had, you wouldn't have come,' Bobby said.

'Why was it so bloody important that I did come anyway? I haven't been invited to Greysham for two years. Why bloody well now?'

'Stop being so wretchedly uncouth!' Annabel's voice, from her place by the window, was raised in a shout.

'Uncouth he may be,' Bobby persisted, 'but the dear boy has a point. Why *has* Hildreth invited us here? Certainly not for the shooting – in my case, at least. You know what I think? I think Hildreth believes there was something funny about Antonio's death, and whatever it was, he thinks one of us was part of it.'

'Don't be so bloody silly,' Giles said. 'How could there be "something funny"? No one pushed the poor sod off his pony, did they? I heard he was too eager for the ball and simply toppled over. It's happened to me several times. Luckily, I never managed to break my neck in the process.'

Bobby eyed him malevolently. 'The autopsy showed he had a heavy concentration of heroin in his system,' he said evenly. 'Very silly thing to do before strenuous exercise, especially when mixed with alcohol.'

'Was he boozed up as well?' Richard Luke asked quietly from a far corner of the room.

'Apparently he had had several glasses of champagne, and the heroin was mixed in it.'

'No one takes heroin that way! You mean he didn't inject it or breathe it in?'

'Not from what the examination showed. The question is whether Antonio mixed in the heroin himself or whether someone did it for him without taking the trouble to tell him.'

'That would be murder,' Luke said. 'I think the combination would have killed him whether he fell or not.'

'Exactly.' Bobby seemed quietly pleased with the conclusion. 'You hated him, Giles,' he went on. 'If you made Antonio his heroin cocktail, be a good chap and own up quickly so we can all go home.'

'Home?' asked Giles. 'I thought we had some other things to talk about?'

The room went silent once more.

I sipped my tea, still standing by the round mahogany table. A brass clock on the mantelpiece ticked laboriously. Giles had obviously blown something – something I wasn't supposed to hear. Even Bobby's normally puffy white cheeks had gone a little pink.

'I'll be in the library,' he said. Slipping out of his chair, he went toward the door. He was limping; he must have been suffering from one of his attacks of gout.

Just as he took hold of the doorhandle, he turned to face us. His mouth was twisted in a sneer as he said, 'The interesting question, of course, is if Hildreth really does believe all this nonsense, why hasn't he simply handed over the whole matter to the police? Very strange, don't you think? The taxpayer provides us with a perfectly good police force, all hot and eager to undertake just this sort of assignment, and Hildreth goes and deprives them of the job by taking the whole thing onto his own shoulders. Very strange.'

No one answered him as he left the room. I was left to ponder on the question of why the whole of this last speech had been addressed directly to me.

CHAPTER FIVE

About an hour later I lay in my bath breathing in the deep scent of pine from the Badedas foam. Usually I connect the smell of Badedas with holidays and relaxation. On this occasion it failed quite to match my mood. I confess I was troubled. I didn't know what on earth to make of this house party and I tried once again to work out what could have been John's motive for organising it.

From my point of view it certainly looked as if it was going to be a less than wholly enjoyable weekend. I shook the foam off my left foot and used my toes to turn on the hot water tap. I considered once more the make-up of my fellow guests; what a rum lot they all were. As John Hildreth had promised, they had one characteristic in common: they had all known Antonio. In fact, with the possible exception of Michael's wife, Lucy, they had each known him very well. Bobby had been his patron, Richard his protegé-cum-employee, Sylvia and Annabel his mistresses, and Giles his rival. As for myself, I had to admit it, I had also been Antonio's mistress, though I preferred to think of it in terms of his having been my lover; certainly during our entire relationship Antonio had given me nothing except, occasionally, his body. I can't remember ever having received so much as a bunch of flowers from him. I, on the other hand, had lavished him for the short duration of our romance with ties and shirts and gold chains and bracelets, anything, in fact, which he could hang round his neck and wrists.

Yes, evidently we each had Antonio in common. But was that all? I tried to think of any other links there might be between us. As it happened, we had all on one occasion been skiing at the same time at Davos, but that had been a coincidence and was unlikely, I guessed, to provide a serious explanation as to why we were all house guests together now.

My mind drifted to Giles Lester's indiscreet remark. The group in the South Room had evidently been taken aback by his outburst. It had made them very uncomfortable, the more so when Bobby Longfellow had so abruptly left the room. Each of them had sat in silence, apparently troubled by his own thoughts, until I could stand it no longer and had gone for a walk in the garden.

I soaped my neck and began to massage the muscles at the top of my shoulder blades. Rather arrogantly, perhaps, I began to sense that I would be central to any drama which might be about to be played out. John had seemed so certain that he needed me. The only question was whether I had been invited down in my professional capacity or as a participant. Either was possible. On the one hand, I was very much part of this set. If you like, they were my people. On and off, I had spent much of my adult life in their company and that of their friends.

On the other hand, John certainly, and Bobby probably, were clearly aware of my connections with the security services. Sadly, these things have a way of getting out to those who are well connected. Needless to say, this was a source of some discomfiture to me. The fewer people who knew what I did, the better. Much of my work involved mixing with the mega-rich and the international smart set, a good proportion of whom I had known socially for a very long time. It could sometimes be a serious handicap when people found out my professional interest in them. The rogues amongst them clammed up and the others just felt awkward. Either way, I was the loser and so, therefore, was the taxpayer. The cases I have cleared up most effectively have usually been those where I have been able to operate totally incognito. There is a Boeing 747 still flying around the world today which would have been blown out of the sky with three hundred and fifty people on board had the would-be assassin known my true identity at the time; but perhaps more of that another time.

To return to the events which are central to this story, I found myself staring into the large gilded mirror hanging beside the bath. I must admit I was not unhappy with what I saw. Without wishing to exaggerate the point, my figure was still of a shape and size which I suspect would have been the envy of many teenagers. There was a freshness about my body, in particular its skin, which was, I suppose, surprising given the buffeting to which it had been subjected over the years. Only I knew how extensive this had been. It is true that I bruise very easily: the slightest fall brings me out in bright blue patches, especially on my arms, legs and bottom. My answer to this has always been to lash out on body lotions and after-bath creams, with which I cover myself from top to toe every day.

I have to admit my body at that time was rather more than just soft and fresh: it was also trained to a very high athletic pitch. I was fitter and more supple than I would have dreamed possible a few years earlier. I owed this not only to the professionalism of my combat instructors, but also, it has to be said, to my own determination always to be prepared to defend myself, especially against strong unfriendly males. To this end, I kept up a daily routine of very complicated exercises, whenever possible ran a fast five miles across country, and crawled twenty lengths of any decent-sized swimming pool I found available.

The only problem with my body at the precise moment I am describing was that it had turned puce with the heat of the bath water. I decided it was time to dry myself and to prepare once again to meet the others.

I stepped onto a sheepskin bathmat, wrapped a large golden-coloured towel around myself, and crossed over to a dressing table on the far side of the room. Still slightly damp, I sat down on a round Georgian stool and began the therapeutic process of stroking a brush through my hair, which I had grown to my shoulders, a little longer than usual. I twisted the ends of my hair into a curl and decided there was little point in agonising further about why such a motley crowd had been gathered together at Greysham. No doubt the good Lord Hildreth would reveal all in his own time which, if he deigned to turn up at all, would be after seven thirty that evening.

The thought of John Hildreth turned my mind to his brother Michael at which the brush strokes, I'm sure, moved a little faster. I also took a decision at that moment about what to wear for the evening.

I made up my mind not, after all, to put on the long silk dress which I had bought at Belville Sassoon, but to switch instead to the three-quarter length salmon pink number with the lowish neckline. Made of cotton, this was a little closer fitting than the other. I got up impulsively from the dressing table and hurried into the adjoining room; as I did so I left a trail of footprints across the white carpet. In the bedroom I opened a large mahogany wardrobe and discovered with some relief that both evening dresses had been pressed and were hanging ready for me to wear.

When some twenty minutes later I entered the drawing room, I knew I was looking pretty good. As it was late summer I had not needed to use too much make-up: a touch of powder over the tan which I had picked up on a recent job in the Mediterranean, and a soft pink lipstick to match the dress. Just before leaving my room I had remembered that I had brought with me my gold and pearl drop earrings and I was pleased that I had; they were exactly right for the occasion.

Three or four groups had gathered separately around the long rectangular room with its three high-backed sofas, flowing red felt curtains and its large marble fireplace. To me the drawing room had always been the grandest and the most awesome feature of the house. Perhaps it was the way that the large ornate gilded mirrors had been arranged around the room, the most formidable of them being a heavily carved Adam original over the mantelpiece. Their total effect was to give a sense of great space and grandeur: one felt one was entering a mini grand salon after the style of one of the classic European palaces, Schönbrun or even Versailles.

As I made my way from the door to the centre of the room, I was aware of being one of the last of the house party to have arrived for dinner. My habit of being a little late for social events is not one I cultivate; I know it irritates several of my friends, especially those who are aware of how punctilious I am when I am working. It's just, I suppose, that these days my job comes first: even when I have left enough time to get ready for going out, my mind still lingers on the day's problems and the allotted time seems to vanish mysteriously.

As I came up to the outer ring of guests, John Hildreth suddenly interposed himself between them and me. He was grinning and sweeping a hand through his hair. Every few moments he very slightly flexed back his shoulders with a strange little twitch. The movement would probably not have been noticeable to someone who had not known him as well as I had. I wondered whether he was in pain. His body sagged and he gave me a rather awkward kiss on the cheek.

'Thanks for coming, Jane,' he said with unexpected warmth. I wondered for a moment whether perhaps he was trying to make up for the hostility towards me of the rest of the party. Then I realised that he probably would not have had the opportunity to sense their mood. It would certainly have been totally out of character for him to have been driven by any sense of guilt, for instance, for not having been around on my arrival. The truth, I concluded, was that he was simply pleased to see me and wanted to show it.

I looked over his shoulder around the room. 'Where's Elizabeth?' I asked.

He hesitated and then said, 'Later; we'll talk about all that later.' For a moment his eyes missed mine and then as they focused themselves on me once more he cheered up.

'Darling, I'm so pleased you've come.'

'I've been here for the last three hours,' I replied.

'Still managed to be late for dinner though.' He raised his eyebrows and lowered the corners of his mouth in a mocking gesture. 'Tut, tut, I don't know how Leyland and I ever put up with it.'

'You didn't,' I said simply and his eyes went into another gyration, this time in the direction of the floor, on which he began to make a circle with his right foot.

'Let me get you a drink,' his voice was more subdued. 'Champagne OK?'

'Champagne would be fine.'

He turned away to look for Leyland and left me to wonder again at the oddness of Elizabeth Hildreth's absence. I had been quite looking forward to the prospect of finding out a bit more about her this weekend. I would have enjoyed also discovering a little more of my own feelings towards John. I knew I wasn't jealous of Elizabeth. If I had ever been, it was well over by this time. In any case I don't think I am the jealous type. I tend to take my relationships with men as they come. Some might say I am too dispassionate. Less cynicism might have brought me more suffering but also perhaps more ecstasy. It might also have made concentration on my work more difficult. No, I'm pretty certain I wasn't jealous of Elizabeth but I was very wary of her. Part of the reason for this may have been the fact that we were so different.

Even physically we were opposites. Elizabeth was not only much taller than I am, her features were sharper, more striking than mine. Her hair was a much deeper gold and she wore darker lipsticks than I ever do. Everything about her was more perfect.

I think it's fair to say, everything was also much harsher. She was nervy and prone to bad headaches. I had heard somewhere that she would sometimes go to bed for several days with what were thought to be migraines. I, on the other hand, am placid almost to a fault, at least on the outside. What goes on deep down inside me I have probably yet fully to find out myself. I have never been psychoanalysed and have no plans to be, but I imagine it would be possible to discover all manner of strange theories as to what makes me tick! Such as why, for instance, I allow myself to end up in so many situations which are undoubtedly physically dangerous. My employment is, after all, a matter of my own personal choice. I don't have to do the job I do. It would not, I suppose, have been hard for me to have found a husband or a lover and to have settled down with him to live quietly ever after, had I particularly wanted that.

John came back carrying two tulip-shaped champagne glasses.

'This should cheer you up,' he said.

'I wasn't miserable.'

'Angry then.'

'Angry?' I raised my right eyebrow.

'About my not meeting you at the front door.'

'My dear John, think nothing of it. It's just that I could have happily used three hours doing things I don't get much time to do these days, like shopping, that's all.'

'That's all right then. As long as you're not angry with me.'

'Not at all, I promise you.' My lack of interest in this particular episode was genuine; anyway, I certainly wasn't going to pander to John's mock humility.

He took hold of my arm and led me towards a corner of the room. I went with him somewhat reluctantly. When he judged we could not be heard by the others, he whispered, 'About Elizabeth.'

'Yes?'

'She's not here.'

'I see that. But why?'

'It's complicated.'

'Things so often are with you, John.'

'Don't be like that. This is different.'

'Has she left you?'

'Possibly.'

'What do the others think about her not being here?'

'They take things like that in their stride; they're a sophisticated bunch – too damned sophisticated sometimes.'

'Oh I see.'

I fell silent but he seemed keen to pursue the matter. 'We agreed to operate together this weekend. She usually keeps her word.'

'Operate' was an odd word to use to describe a

husband and wife entertaining together in their own home, but I let it pass and said simply, 'So she's let you down.'

'There may be some explanation.' Suddenly he seemed to grow tired of the subject of Elizabeth. 'Do you mind sitting next to me at dinner tonight?' His manner seemed to have become rather distracted.

'Not at all,' I said. 'As a matter of fact I had rather hoped I would. There are an awful lot of questions I want to ask. What's more, I have to tell you I'm not madly enthused by the rest of your house party.'

He did not appear to have heard what I had said. He was looking at me more intently than I had ever known him to do before.

'I had forgotten just how beautiful you are,' he said.

'Thank you, kind sir, but don't get too carried away. What's past is over. There is no way I ever want to revive it. I enjoyed being married to you for a time, John, but it's finished. Besides, I've grown up and changed. It would never be the same.'

He looked at me in silence for a moment and smiled. 'Quite so. I think we had better lead the way into dinner, otherwise Leyland will start becoming stroppy. He's changed too, you know. You would think he owned the place these days. I'm quite serious. Come on, I'll grab you another glass of champagne as we go in. You can drink it at the table.'

He left me and began to usher the other guests towards the double doors on the north side of the drawing room. There was a restlessness about John which I had never seen before. I watched him closely as he fussed us into dinner. His nervousness was out of character.

Giles Lester seemed to notice it as well. He leant his tall, well-proportioned body against the frame of the door, his eyes half closed and an empty champagne glass in his left hand. A lock of hair fell across his forehead. He placed an arm around John's shoulder.

'What's the hurry, old man?' Giles's voice, tipsy-sounding already, rose above the general chatter. 'Not like you to worry about keeping Leyland waiting. Is he working to rule or something?' The idea of a militant semi-striking Leyland seemed to amuse him and he began to laugh loudly. John appeared to shrug off his arms. The rest of us shuffled past Giles, who moved to a position of guard-like attention. He would probably have made a good soldier. He certainly had the physique for it.

The dining room, when we entered it, was in almost total darkness. The curtains of the three windows overlooking the west lawn were undrawn, but the autumn light had faded, presumably so fast as to have caught Leyland unawares: he had not yet arranged for the candles down the centre of the table to be lit. So it was with some difficulty that we began to hunt for our place names.

As John had already told me that I was to sit next to him at the far end of the table, I was able to find my place to his left with comparative ease. Bobby Longfellow was already sitting down, to my right, his napkin tucked into his collar and splayed out across the front of his bulging chest. He made no attempt to rise as I approached him. As a matter of fact, he failed to acknowledge my arrival at all. He seemed to be in some sort of a trance. His slightly bloated bald baby face remained expressionless as he stared straight ahead across the table.

He took no more interest in Annabel Silvester when she arrived a few moments later and sat herself down noisily on his left.

'You're not much of a gentleman, I must say,' I heard her declaim, with a directness and a loudness I could never have matched in a thousand years. She might just as well not have bothered. Bobby was not to be so easily engaged.

Bobby's taste in women was known to be a little 'different'. It would be interesting to see as the evening progressed whether Annabel managed to make any headway with him. Rumour had it that he liked noisy ladies, in which case there was a chance that Annabel might fit the bill exactly. According to Giles Lester she needed to shave her face once a fortnight. I could imagine that rather appealing to Bobby as well.

I could just make out through the gloom the slight figure of Richard Luke sliding himself down beside Annabel. Immediately she gave up the struggle with Bobby and seemed to fall on top of the wretched Luke. He must have said something funny, speaking as always through his front teeth in a tone which was little higher than a whisper. Annabel opened her mouth wide and burst into loud laughter, flinging her left arm simultaneously around Richard's neck and so almost crushing his little head.

Next to Luke and at the end of the table opposite John Hildreth, a place had been laid but was unoccupied. I supposed it had been left empty in the hope that Elizabeth might put in a last minute appearance. As if to confirm the point, Leyland glided up behind John and whispered in his ear. They both peered to the end of the table and John nodded. This evidently satisfied Leyland, who retreated with a smile fixed to his lips and his head cocked to one side, as it had been on my arrival.

It was at this point that I saw Michael Hildreth. He had slipped unusually quietly and almost unnoticed into his seat opposite Richard Luke (as far away from where I was sitting as it was possible to be). It was the first time I had seen him since my arrival at Greysham. I was rather pleased to be sitting on the other side of the table from him, far enough away so that I could look at him without having to speak to him.

His presence made me feel uneasy. He was astonishingly good-looking, more so tonight than ever. He had grown his hair to a length which suited him perfectly, it cascaded at the back in well-groomed layers just over his white silk shirt collar. His bottle green velvet smoking jacket had been tailored precisely to fit the contours of his wide shoulders and the tapering lines of his torso. His boyish, firmly chiselled face shone with a summer tan, contrasting magnificently with the white lace of his dress shirt.

'To be admired but not touched,' I reminded myself. Michael was dangerous: he was rich; he was clever; he was gorgeous; and by all accounts he was totally unaware of his capacity to hurt. I wasn't sure whether this was through naivete, lack of sensitivity, or plain ruthlessness.

The only person in the world to whom he appeared to defer was his brother John. Again, it was unclear to me whether this was out of affection and regard for an elder brother, or from the sullen frustration of one who has been deprived of a vast inheritance by our peculiar system of primogeniture. Michael was an enigma, but a damnably attractive one.

Continuing round the table, on Michael's left sat Sylvia Richards. Antonio had been correct about her. She was very pretty. She wore a pale green chiffon dress which barely covered her top half and was see-through. Her fair hair fell in ringlets to her shoulders. She wore deep red lipstick, which suited her. Her eyes, which were round and blue, were her special feature. She was right to accentuate them with a dark eye-shadow. I knew several men who found Sylvia's eyes, and no doubt other bits of her, irresistible.

Next to Sylvia was Giles Lester, who was also, therefore, almost opposite me. He pulled a strand of

Sylvia's hair as he sat down and winked at me, apparently having totally forgotten his behaviour to me earlier on that afternoon. I was beginning to think that master Giles must be a little schizoid. I had heard it said of him before that he had an infinite capacity to forget his own rudeness. I wished there were easy ways of crushing men like Giles Lester; crushing them without perhaps totally obliterating them. It has to be admitted they add colour, might as well say it – sex appeal – to the events they attend. I was struck by the differing good looks of Giles and Michael. Giles was a few years older. His hair, though fair, was darker than Michael's and certainly shorter. Michael's face was more boyish, his cheeks pinker; he was generally the more flamboyant of the two.

Despite this, I felt Michael's temperament was likely to be the more consistent, even predictable. I won't say he was the 'more trustworthy' of the two. The term is pretty meaningless out of context. To know whether you trust someone you have first to decide what it is you want to do with them. Do you want to make money? Or fight a war? Or make love to them? Each demands totally different and sometimes incompatible qualities of trust. I did not know Michael well enough to be able to make up my mind about whether he possessed any of them. I was pretty sure that Giles Lester was not over-blessed with many trustworthy qualities. He might possibly have had certain pretensions as a lover, but there was no way I felt that I would wish to trust my body too close to his. I had no doubt he was practised, but I suspected he might also be soiled.

Michael, on the other hand, certainly had had several girlfriends to my personal knowledge, but I liked to think of him, perhaps a little over-generously, as having a certain self-control, a pride in himself, amounting no doubt at times to narcissism. He was certainly not displeased with his own looks and I am sure he cultivated his physique, while I doubted whether Giles bothered to 'look after himself' beyond playing sports very hard and extremely well when it suited him to do so. He certainly drank and smoked too much. You felt with Michael that his passion for polo, for instance, was part of a cult. He wanted to stretch himself. As he grew older he might even become a bore about his need to take exercise.

I took a sip from my half-empty champagne glass. I was rather enjoying having the two of them in my sights.

To Giles's left, and therefore on John Hildreth's right (and exactly opposite me), sat Michael's wife, Lucy. The only thing that appeared real about her was her hair, which was dark brown and fell straight to the middle of her back. The rest of her seemed to be translucent. Somehow one felt she would be impossible to touch.

Her expressionless white face with its little snub nose was fixed like the face of a statue. Her eyes, too, were transfixed and stared past mine to a point on the wall behind me. Her long, white dress with its puffy short sleeves was actually rather pretty, but on her merely served to make her more ghost-like. My overwhelming emotion towards her was one of pity. I only wished that I could find a way of getting through to her. I felt that shrouded beneath her sad, misty surface something beautiful might be hidden. There must have been some reason why Michael had married her. It would certainly not have been from any shortage of choice on his part.

Lucy had been the last to arrive at the table and as she did so I noticed Leyland emerge from the shadows from where he must have been watching us. He glided to Lucy's place and gently pulled out her chair for her. When she had sat down, he eased her chair with great care towards the table. Neither spoke a word to the other and yet I had an instant sense of there being some sort of a bond between them which went beyond that of the relationship between a member of the family and the staff. There seemed to be a certain rhythm in their movement. It was also noticeable that no other woman present had received this particular touch of courtesy from Leyland.

As soon as Lucy was safely seated, Leyland faded again into the dark recess of the room. He re-emerged a moment later wielding two bottles.

'Shall I pour the white wine now, my Lord?' he asked. John Hildreth did not immediately appear to hear him.

'Shall I serve the wine?' Leyland repeated.

'Yes, yes, go ahead, but check whether anyone wants any more champagne.'

It was unlike John to appear so distracted. However, he seemed to pull himself together when he added, 'Oh, and Leyland, could we have the candles lit? I can't see a damned thing.'

It was true; the light had suddenly faded to the point where we were in darkness. For a moment no-one talked; I vividly remember the strange sense of eeriness which hung over us. Something suddenly moved beside me and with a spasm of well-trained reflex I jerked my elbow towards my stomach. I realised then that the disturbance had been caused by Bobby Longfellow tucking the corner of his table napkin more firmly into his collar and poking my ribs with his elbow as he did so. My jumpiness had been for no real cause.

As Leyland leant across the centre of the table and began to light the candles, it became possible to identify the thin slices of smoked salmon set before us on plates which were ringed in deep blue and gold. I thought I recognised them as having been given to

John and me as a wedding present, but my memory may have been playing tricks with me. At any rate, Bobby Longfellow began to attack the smoked salmon with a knife and fork and we all followed his lead.

Shadows of a line of heads flickered on the wall opposite me. No one seemed to want to talk. The gloom even seemed to have infected Giles Lester; head down, he picked at the fish as intently as the rest of us.

Much to my surprise, it was my neighbour who broke the silence. With a mouth full of salmon, Bobby Longfellow suddenly growled, 'What we want to know, John, is why we are all here. I've got a lot going on in my constituency this weekend. Yet you insisted we come. It's not convenient, but I have put myself at your disposal. Now what's it all about?'

Everyone, including Lucy Hildreth, turned towards John. His face was very red and he was sweating. His newly acquired double chin sparkled in the candle-light. In the past I had only seen him sweat properly after he had been playing polo. It wasn't as if it was particularly hot in the room; in fact, I think I remember shivering slightly as Bobby spoke. With his right hand, John swept back into place a strand of hair which had fallen cross his forehead. For a moment he looked at me as if for reassurance. Then he began to speak.

'I have to tell you, one of us around this table kills people. When he or she acts, it is done with a special type of ruthlessness. The killing is carried out unexpectedly and in such a way as to make it almost impossible to detect. Those who are closest to the killer, those who are friends, have most to fear. Our task this weekend is to find out which one of us it is. We shall have to move fast before another murder is committed.'

I could see the whites of John's eyes; they seemed to be straining to peer deeper into the gloom as he continued, 'I am in no doubt that the next intended victim is also sitting in this room tonight. You see, there is a clear pattern which leads from Antonio's death straight to the group of us sitting here. What is so frightening is that we are tied up in this ghastly business together; yes, we're all in it. Each linked with the other: hunter and hunted; victim and killer. The difficulty is in separating one from the other.'

CHAPTER SIX

John's words had an interesting variety of effects on the guests seated around the dinner table. I studied these reactions as carefully as I could, given the poor light thrown out by the candles. Bobby went on eating. A small piece of smoked salmon fell from his fork onto the napkin hanging from his neck. Michael stared at his plate, apparently overcome with uncharacteristic embarrassment. Annabel whispered something indistinctly to Richard, whose face was invisible from where I was sitting. Sylvia was clearly on the point of bursting into tears.

It was Lucy's reaction which was for me the most surprising. For the first time that evening her eyes became alive. Her large black pupils, which until that moment had been set like small rocks, began to sparkle. Suddenly there was a new beauty in her pale face. For a moment I thought she was about to speak. Staring directly at John, she opened her mouth and then seemed to change her mind. Noiselessly she closed her lips again and the shine in her eyes faded. It would, of course, have been of enormous interest to me to know what had prompted these sudden changes in mood. She could not possibly have been elated by John's remarks; I could only assume that her temporary animation must have been caused by something like anger. Whatever the cause, for the first time

I had had a taste of her unexploited physical qualities. When she came to life Lucy Hildreth was a very beautiful woman.

Next to her, Giles Lester went red and was the first to make a recognisable noise.

'Bloody ridiculous,' he said loudly.

'What is?' John asked quietly.

'That any one of us should have taken it into his head to murder Antonio.'

'You once threatened to,' John said.

Giles was prevented from answering back by an interruption from Bobby Longfellow.

'The bit I don't understand,' he said, 'is how you can claim to have narrowed it down to us. The man had literally hundreds of enemies.'

'That was the easy part,' John replied without hesitation.

Bobby's eyes narrowed. There was a power behind them which I had not noticed before. When he spoke it was almost a command.

'Go on,' he said.

John stared straight back at him with a surface calm. I wondered whether I was the only one who noticed that his right hand had screwed his table napkin into a tiny ball and that his knees were shaking under the table.

'Antonio was blackmailing you,' he said.

'Was he just? All of us or some of us or just me?' Bobby, too, now seemed on the verge of losing his cool; he was becoming angry.

'That I'm not sure,' John replied. 'Certainly you and Richard and Giles; I don't know about the two girls.'

As if objecting to John's uncertainty about her, Annabel cried, 'You're guessing. The whole thing's outrageous.' Her chubby, normally rosy face had gone white.

'I'm doing rather better than that,' John said. 'You

don't underestimate the contact I had with Antonio, do you, Bobby?' There was a bitterness in his voice.

Bobby raised his right eyebrow. 'Elizabeth?' he asked.

John nodded.

'How long have you known?' Bobby persisted.

'About what?'

'That Elizabeth and Antonio were lovers.'

John reached for the china box in front of him, took out a cigarette and lit it with a silver table lighter.

'Almost from the start,' he said, inhaling deeply.

'What a funny man you are, John,' Bobby said. 'A bit kinky, I would say. For eighteen months you knew your beautiful, if slightly over-sexed, wife was having it off with Antonio and you did nothing about it. Very strange.' Bobby shook his head in disbelief.

John moved back in his seat and tried to cross his legs but found it impossible to do so under the table. He drew on his cigarette and shifted himself again uncomfortably. He looked tired and much older than his age.

'She was getting tired of him,' he said uneasily. Bobby watched him intently. His voice when he spoke was clearer and firmer than I had ever heard it.

'How do you know, dear boy?' he asked.

'Elizabeth and I still talk a lot. We have never lost touch.'

I thought the 'still' sounded rather pathetic, and I found myself beginning to feel a bit sorry for John.

'Has she talked much about Antonio?' The question came from Richard Luke – his first contribution to the evening's proceedings.

'In the end, yes.'

'Before his death?' The tone of Richard's voice was quite a contrast to Bobby's, polite and reserved.

'Yes.'

'Now I understand,' said Bobby, and so brought

Richard's short line of questioning to an end. The room fell silent. Michael ran his index finger around the rim of his champagne glass; then he lifted the glass and drank it empty. He had said nothing since he had sat down at the table.

The peace was eventually broken by Giles Lester. 'So Elizabeth was about to ditch Antonio. Well, well.'

'I didn't say that,' John said without looking at the speaker. He flicked a speck of ash from his right sleeve and coughed. I found his nervousness interesting. It made him seem less impregnable and therefore, I suppose, more attractive. Richard Luke reopened the questioning this time. There was now an almost mocking edge to his voice.

'I thought I heard you say that Elizabeth was growing tired of Antonio.' My respect for Richard was growing. There was a toughness about him which I hadn't noticed before.

'She was becoming tired of his style of living, and I can't say that I blame her.' John's normally gravelly voice was becoming higher pitched; it was beginning to sound defensive. Nor I suspected, was I the only one of those present to notice this.

Inevitably, perhaps, Bobby was the first to exploit the new opportunity.

'What I don't understand is why Elizabeth would want to spoil her randy affair with Antonio just when he was presumably giving her a lot of fun. They say Elizabeth is very demanding and that Antonio was able to come up with most of the goods. Why put all that at risk by shopping the man? It simply doesn't make sense, unless, that is, she had found herself someone else.'

'Elizabeth certainly knows how to pull in the boys,' giggled Sylvia. Tears were still glistening in her eyes; she clearly had a rather remarkable capacity for quick mood changes.

Bobby had twisted his chair so that he was now facing John in open confrontation.

'Is that it, John? She's found someone else, your Elizabeth? Quite a woman, isn't she? Bit tough on you, though, dear boy, seeing that you still fancy her like crazy. Can't say I blame you. She's very beautiful.'

He was speaking more rapidly than I had ever heard him speak before. He clearly had the capability to change pace, which has been the characteristic of all the good interrogators I have known.

Suddenly John's mask of calm fell away and he exploded. 'Blast your vulgarity and your impertinence,' he shouted. 'Yes, she does have another man – probably an army of them for all I know. Now do you feel better? You should certainly have enough to satisfy your loathsome gossip columnist friends, Bobby. Perhaps on reflection you should ask her to show you some pictures of what she does; she'd probably like that, and so, I have no doubt, would you. She'd probably give them to you without charge. I think all of Elizabeth's favours are still free.' A tear from the corner of his eye rolled down the side of his face and was followed by another.

'I must say this is interesting,' Bobby said.

'Very juicy,' Sylvia added.

'What I want to know is where this all leaves us,' Richard said.

'If you're John Hildreth, in one hell of a mess,' Giles answered. 'Poor old John, you seem to have taken on too much for your own good in Elizabeth. Much better in the event to have stuck with little Jane over there. Not such a goer, perhaps, but very pretty and perfectly clean, I'm sure.'

At the mention of my name, John turned to stare at me. As he did so, he seemed to regain some of his composure.

'Where it leaves us is where I began,' he said. 'With

the blackmail. What we need do is find out exactly which ones of you were regularly paying large sums of money to Antonio in return for his silence, and whether as a result he was murdered, and if so, by whom. I have a pretty shrewd idea about all these matters.'

'And you've brought Jane down to help you prove it?' Richard asked.

Bobby suddenly stood up, his rounded stomach pressing against the edge of the table. He turned to John and stared at him for a moment. There was a cold anger in his eyes when he said, 'I don't think I have ever heard such appalling fantasy in my life. You should see a doctor, John. You're living in a world of your own. Don't take it out on us that Elizabeth cheated on you. Don't forget that you had the best motive of all for killing Antonio.'

CHAPTER SEVEN

Not surprisingly, perhaps, I found it impossible to sleep that night. The conversation at the dinner table, if 'conversation' is the right word for a verbal duel, had taken its toll. My brain had become too active for sleep. John's behaviour had not made any sense at all. None of his half suggestions and innuendo had seemed to add up to anything of substance. There had been no real logic to what he had been saying. Above all, he had given no motive at all – not so much as a scrap – for the suggestion that Antonio was blackmailing the members of the houseparty whom John had so mysteriously gathered together. If John was even half right in his accusations – and he had said nothing which so far as I could see would be given five minutes of a judge's time in a court of law – the obvious question was, what was it that Antonio had known about Bobby and the rest for which they would pay him good money to keep to himself? And the innuendo of that was that one of them had finally found a way of killing him. No one at dinner, least of all John, had even touched on the subject.

All this, therefore, left – for the time being at least – a much more interesting issue than that of who was blackmailing whom and for what: what was John Hildreth up to? What on earth had led my former husband to devise this bizarre weekend? If he genuinely felt so strongly about the Antonio business, why had he not simply telephoned the nearest police station? Or for that matter, if he had wanted to keep the whole matter close to his chest, possibly in some sort of attempt to protect his relationship with Elizabeth, why had he not put me more fully in the picture?

After two hours of tossing and turning, trying to make some sort of sense of all this, I switched on the light beside my bed and, on an impulse, pushed back the bedclothes and swung my feet onto the floor. Getting up, I crossed over to the door and was relieved to find I had remembered to turn the key in the lock before going to bed. For a moment I stood shivering in my nightdress. The window curtains had been blown open and a strong draught was flowing across the room.

When I returned to my bed, I decided I would finish off the report on my last job. This had been a simple matter of tracking down an Irishman, whose habit of providing crucial information on a regular basis to the IRA was unwelcome to the government, especially as at one time he had been quite a useful police contact. I had not on this occasion had to do much travelling since Mr X had settled himself down with a girlfriend in a house in south London. The only tricky bit in the whole operation had been whisking the client into our care and custody while simultaneously dissuading the girlfriend from raising the alarm too quickly with the IRA command. She remains a free lady to this day, I think married and living in California, because of the way she co-operated with the disappearing act we arranged for her. I fear it took some pretty brutal talking by this writer to achieve it. The effect, however, was that we were able to make a series of further arrests in Belfast during the next twenty-four hours as a result of what we learnt from Mr X.

The case had had a beginning, a middle and an end, which was by no means always true of my work. The style of the report could therefore be concise and factual. There was no need for speculative analysis which might enable someone else to pick up the matter again at a future date. I was as sure as I could be that Mr X was drained of all information which was likely to be of any immediate use to us. I expected that the men we had inside the prison he had been sent to for twenty years would be able to keep an eye on him in the future.

I had been writing for about half an hour when my concentration was suddenly interrupted by a low knock at my door. I put down my pen and folded, into an eighth of its true size, the lined government foolscap paper on which I had been writing. I leant over the side of my bed and placed the paper into the toe of a pink mohair slipper. The knock repeated itself.

'Who is it?' I whispered.

'Me.' The reply was so soft that I was barely able to make out whose voice it was. It was only by a process of association that I could half-guess its identity. I had been expecting him to make some sort of a move like this.

'John,' I said. 'What do you want?'

'It's time to talk, Jane. May I come in?'

'I'm half asleep. Won't tomorrow do?'

'No, no, I promise you it's urgent. I wouldn't have bothered you like this if it could wait.'

I had slipped a blue woollen cardigan over my nightdress and was now putting on my dressing gown. 'I'm beginning to find all this a little wearisome, John. If the weekend goes on much further like this, I think I may well go home before Sunday.'

During the course of this half-whispered conversation, I had tested the weight of a small wooden upright chair and had carried it to a position near the door.

I turned off the light in my room before opening the door. He was leaning back against the wall on the opposite side of the passage. A strand of black hair hung down his left cheek. He was still dressed in his dinner jacket, his black bow tie was skewed to the side. Hung loosely around his neck was a white silk evening scarf, his monogram discreetly embroidered in white silk at one end.

He swayed slightly on his feet – evidently he had been drinking. 'OK,' I said. 'You'd better come in. It doesn't look as though you're going to be able to stand much longer.'

He entered my room. I closed the door behind him and switched on the light. As I did so he sank onto my bed.

I pulled up a small button-back chair and sat on it. He shook off a pair of black patent leather shoes and dangled his feet over the side of my bed.

'Which one of us should start?' he asked. 'I'm sure there must be masses of questions you want to ask me.' His voice was rough and he slurred his words.

When I made no response he said, 'Let's begin with Elizabeth, then.'

'I thought it might be Elizabeth,' I said. 'I don't want to get involved in this, John. You married her.' I wondered for a moment where the glamorous Elizabeth would be sleeping tonight and with whom.

John began to cry. 'I love her so much. God, I love her,' he sobbed. Some women are revolted by the sight of a man weeping. I am not. A man who cries has a sensitivity about him which I find attractive. On this occasion, however, I was not quite so inclined to be sympathetic.

'Why not ring her up first thing tomorrow morning?' I suggested. 'Tell her what a lovely time we are all having and how much we all miss her and what even greater fun it would be if she joined us.'

The sarcasm was lost on him. 'Impossible. It's too late to ring her.' This thought seemed to help him to recover his self-control. He wiped away his tears with the back of his right hand. He paused for a moment, looking straight at me, and then in a voice which was much firmer he said, 'Whatever happens, Jane, I want you to take this case on.'

The idea did not appeal to me at all. I was by no means sure, even, that there was anything for me to do, other than perhaps to find John Hildreth a good psychiatrist. In order not to upset him further, I simply said, 'There's nothing to go on yet.'

'There will be,' he replied. 'Don't worry about that. There will be.' His eyes, which were usually mocking and sometimes seductive, were now lifeless and out of focus, as though he was observing me from a distance. He shook his head as if to clear his mind.

'What made her do it, for Christ's sake? Why did she have to leave me for that Dago? I gave her everything she wanted, everything.' The irony of the subject in my presence seemed to have escaped him. 'What can he possibly have had that I don't? At least, when he was dead I thought she would come back. You do understand, don't you, Jane?'

I was beginning to suspect that I did.

'Anyway, it doesn't really matter now, does it? God, I've been such a fool.'

Then, suddenly, his mood changed. He jumped from the bed onto the floor. For a moment he stood over me menacingly. His eyes were bloodshot. His movement had caught me by surprise. I realised that the chair I had placed by the door as a weapon was now out of reach. It had been careless of me, and I must say out of character to have lost contact with it.

'What the hell am I going to do?' He was shouting.

I stared back into his red eyes. For a moment there was a total silence between us, then I said, 'Come on,

John, it's time you were back in your own bed.'

I got out of my chair and knelt in front of him. Slowly I stood up, my face level with his chest. I took his hand and led him to the door. He paused on the threshold. Very strangely, he held out both his hands. I thought he was asking me to come with him. Then in a faint whisper, he said, 'Jane, we're part of the same show, you know.' He seemed to feel that I had failed to grasp his meaning and that he needed to drive the point home. 'We work for the same office. Has that sunk in? What I am onto with this lot is definitely for our office – absolutely not for the police; that's very important. I know I've had a little too much to drink, but I hope I am making myself clear, its foreign policy stuff, Jane.'

I stared straight back at him, showing absolutely no emotion, as I have been taught to do. His hands, which remained outstretched, were sweating. The dampness on them shimmered in the half light.

'I told the Office I wouldn't go through with this one without you,' he said. 'I specifically requested them to let me have you. It's going to be tough. I told them I'm not up to it on my own. You see, I know you're good: the lads are always talking about you. You probably don't even realise yourself what a reputation you have'. He hesitated.

I thought he was about to go, when a further idea seemed to occur to him. He appeared to strain for a moment, to form his words into a coherent pattern; then he said, 'I should be in a position to brief you fully in the morning. It's not just that I will be sober then. There's someone who has said they want to see me before I turn in tonight. I have a feeling they may be of help. The dinner this evening flushed it out as I thought it might. I'm not just a pretty face, Jane; still got a bit up here.' He tapped his head with his fore-finger and gave an unnatural grin. Then he turned round and disappeared into the night.

I shut the door of my bedroom very quietly and went back to my bedside table. I picked up my clock and was surprised to see that it said two-fifteen. I had had no idea it was so late. I set the alarm for five and put the clock back on the table.

I had made up my mind to leave before the house woke up. The last thing I wanted to do was to go along with John's request to become further involved in whatever he was up to – not, at least without direct ruling from above. One thing was for sure: I was in no mood at all to play games with him. Nor, frankly, could I readily believe that he was a member of the department, though of course this would have to be checked as soon as possible.

If, on the other hand, I was wrong, and John was in some way mixed up in official business, then in my view it would be quite inappropriate for me to be further involved. I was far too close to all the personalities. My former marriage to John ruled me out for a start; besides, I felt a new sympathy towards him which made matters even more complicated especially as I was forming my suspicions about his role in Antonio's death. There was no doubt he had become very unstable; he might even be mentally ill. I doubted now whether his unhappiness about Elizabeth fully explained what was going on inside him. I was beginning to feel it much more likely to have something to do with Antonio's death. This had not been my view at the start of the weekend, but I could no longer totally ignore his obsession with what he seemed honestly to believe was the Argentinian's murder. All this and the need to talk to the office at the earliest opportunity made it doubly important for me to leave as quickly as possible.

I turned off the bedside light. Then, as an afterthought, I stretched out my arm to feel for the clock. I wanted to be sure that I had pulled out the alarm button so that there would be no doubt of my being woken an hour before sunrise.

His behaviour over dinner, the dark hints about foreign policy plots, the accusations of blackmail had to be his attempts to divert attention away from himself.

Why had he said it was too late to ring Elizabeth? Surely it was not possible that he had killed her as well?

CHAPTER EIGHT

It was still dark when the alarm rang. I must have slept for two hours at the most. I shivered in the night air as I got out of bed. When I had fully dressed, I packed the few things I had decided to take with me.

I went across to the half-open window and tried to make an assessment of the distance to the ground. It was too dark to work out the height accurately and I decided it would be unwise to climb down that way. Instead, I picked up my suitcase and carried it out onto the landing. I remember pausing to listen for the sound of any movement. It had become important to me for my departure to go undetected. I didn't want to defend my actions to anyone, especially not to John. I waited for some time to be sure that the house was still fully asleep. When I was certain about this, I began to move towards the main staircase.

My plan was to make for the stables, where I assumed Leyland had arranged for my car to be garaged. When I had lived at Greysham the keys to guests' cars had always been hung on hooks in the far lefthand corner of the stables. I could only hope that this practice was still continued.

Stupidly, I had not kept my spare keys with me. There are techniques for starting cars without the use of the ignition key, but they are messy and I had no wish to practise my off-beat mechanical skills on this particular occasion. I had to trust also that no new system for locking the front door had been installed. Again, it would be a nuisance to have to start picking locks at this time in the morning.

The main staircase at Greysham is wide and made of thick dark oak. It is constructed in two parts. You descend eastwards from the first floor to a half landing from which the stairs reverse in direction, falling from east to west. At the bottom, they connect with the north-south passage by which, if you turn left, you reach the hall and the front door.

As I searched in the darkness with my right foot for the edge of the stairs, I knew at once that it was going to be impossible to leave the house in complete silence. To confirm this, there was a nasty squeak as soon as I put pressure on the first step. I began to descend slowly and very cautiously towards the half-landing. But despite all my care, it was as if my feet were pressing on a field of mini landmines. The creaking and cracking was horrendous. It seemed impossible that anyone could continue sleeping through this. I began to feel that at any moment the entire household would appear at their bedroom doors to watch my descent. Somehow I reached the half landing apparently without rousing anyone. I paused on the flat surface.

For a moment the house was silent again, and then I distinctly heard the click of a door opening on the ground floor. I decided to increase the pace of my movement down the second flight of stairs. As I did so, the groaning beneath my feet grew louder. At last I felt the firmness of the ground floor. This time there was no mistaking the sound of a door closing downstairs. I had no choice but to ignore it. Taking a firm grip on my suitcase, I turned to the left. The passage was so dark I could not see my hands. I remember regretting that I had not set my alarm for half an hour later. It would have been helpful to have been able to guide myself by the first grey of morning light.

I knew there was a table which stood against the left-hand wall some yards down the passage. I began to move slowly towards this landmark.

And then I tripped and fell badly, that is to say heavily, onto my stomach. I am not clumsy and I do not lose my balance easily. I knew at the moment of falling that there must have been an obstruction. As I went down I let go of the suitcase, which landed with a crash in front of me. For a moment I lay face down on the floor, breathing deeply. Then I stretched out my right arm to try to get my bearings. As I did so, my hand pressed itself against cold tissue, which from long experience I recognised instantly as human skin.

Human flesh, when it is alive, is warm and sensual. When it is dead it is like plasticine. This was dead. I felt the mouth, then the teeth, and the hair. I remember pinching my buttocks, as we are taught to do in the service if we think there is any chance of losing consciousness through shock.

I crawled away from the body down the passage, to where I knew there was a light switch. When I turned it on, I saw that the body lying on its back near the foot of the stairs was that of John Hildreth. He lay peacefully with his arms folded across his chest as if he were sleeping. His head had rolled over slightly to the right. His eyes were open. They had the mocking quality in death which they had so often had in life.

He was clothed in his dinner-jacket trousers and dress shirt; the jacket itself was missing. I remember noting that his black bow tie was now perfectly in place.

I have to admit that my overwhelming initial reaction to seeing him lying there was a purely emotional one. It might not have been good police work but I could not help myself. I rushed to his body and knelt beside it. I twisted the head so that it was straight and raised it into my lap. Then I kissed the open lips. I remember tasting the salt of what must have been my own tears.

Then I saw the note sticking out from the clutch of his left hand. I opened the fingers and removed a type-written sheet. I recognised the unusual italic typeface of John's typewriter which he used for nearly all his personal correspondence. John had never been one for writing by hand. The typewriter and the dictating machine had stopped his dyslexia from being any serious handicap to him. The note was short and very much to the point.

I killed Antonio. You see, I couldn't bear any longer what was going on between him and Elizabeth. It was horrible. The irony is that had I stuck with Jane none of this would have happened. She's a proper little woman of the world now and good luck to her. Life for me has become too complicated. It's time to do what used to be called 'the decent thing'. So cheerio, my dears. Try to remember me as not all bad. John Hildreth.

His signature was written in black ink in his usual awkward scrawl.

I read the note twice before folding it into four and putting it into my skirt pocket.

John's unconfident, slightly ersatz bravado which I had often found attractive in him, lingered over him in death. I looked into his eyes and knew that, for this moment at least, I loved him again.

And then the policewoman in me took over. The perfect positioning of the body and the faint drag marks on the carpet – it all pointed against suicide. Despite the note I was sure that John had not taken his own life. I felt that the cause of death would probably turn out to be a lethal overdose of a poison such as asonide potassium, although I had noticed a slight bruising around the neck which the autopsy might show to have some significance.

For the first time since my arrival at Greysham Park, I took on my professional role of killer-hunter. With John's death, there was now no way that I could stand aloof. It would, of course, be for others to decide the extent to which I would become officially involved.

My first duty was to check John's credentials with the office. Rightly or wrongly, my chiefs like to know about a departmental casualty before the police become involved. This is especially so when a death takes place outside the immediate reach of the Metropolitan Police, with whom we have exceptionally close informal ties. John had claimed to be one of our agents and this at least needed to be verified before his body was handed over to the local police, which would be Gloucestershire, the smallest force in the country. I took the decision temporarily to hide the body while I contacted the duty officer at the shop. Otherwise, someone else might stumble over it and call the police before I could speak to my office.

I remembered there was a cupboard under the stairs. In the past this had been very rarely used and then only for purposes such as storing drink when we gave a large party. As I had hoped, the cupboard when I reached it was not only unlocked but also empty. There was no sign of cleaning equipment or hoovers to indicate that it was in any kind of regular use.

It was not the first time I had moved a dead body, but I had never before carried the corpse of someone I had known and loved. It sounds trite, but there is a very great difference. Handling an unknown body is usually a pretty inanimate act, almost like lifting the carcase of an animal. Dealing with the remains of someone you knew when he was alive is quite different; you become deeply aware of the departure of the spirit. For some people this is the most poignant religious experience of all. It is certainly a great shock to the system. In fact, I suspect it was more the effect of the trauma I was going through than the actual weight of John's body which made it such hard work for me to move it. Somehow, however, I did manage to drag it the twenty or so feet from the place where it had evidently been laid with some care to a temporary sepulchre under the stairs.

Once I had placed him in the cupboard and set my suitcase beside him, I returned to the passage and switched off the light. I looked at the luminous dial of my watch: five twenty-five. I had left my bedroom less than twenty minutes earlier.

Again I listened for the sound of movement, but this time there was total silence. I began carefully to retrace my steps up the stairs towards my bedroom. I heard a dog bark in the distance from the direction of the stables. I remember wishing that I had my Smith & Wesson gun strapped around my middle. I would have felt happier to have been armed.

At last I could feel the handle of the door to my room. I twisted it slowly and let myself in. I turned the key in the lock and switched on the light. The room appeared to be as I had left it, though I thought I remembered closing the doors of the wardrobe, which had now swung open. My two evening dresses were hanging inside, lifeless. They seemed to me like two bodies swinging from a gallows. I sensed I was beginning to lose my self-control. Fortunately I was experienced enough to know that the best counter-measure to this is to keep oneself active.

I sat down on my bed and lifted the telephone. The line was dead. I doubted whether this was accidental.

For the first time I sensed I was working against someone who, if not necessarily professional, was certainly thorough.

CHAPTER NINE

There had been a lot of rain during the summer and the harvest had been late that year. As I drove back from Stow-on-the-Wold, where I had managed to place my call through a public telephone, the smoke from the previous day's stubble burning blended with the early morning mist. It was going to be a fine autumn day. Clumps of trees loomed over sweeping Cotswold fields. The dark greens of the month before had turned into gold and shades of brown and even crimson. Beautifully plumed male pheasants and tawny females clustered on the wet grass at the side of the road. Against this rich rolling landscape the events of the previous night seemed unreal, even slightly absurd.

It had, of course, been impossible to have a proper talk with the office on an open line; but I formed the view that they were requesting me to stay on at Greysham for a little longer. Despite indirectly asking for it, I was given no further information about John Hildreth or of any connection he may have had with the service. I had clearly indicated that I needed guidance on this point, and had been given the reply, 'No more news. It's been so nice talking to you, dear.' The voice had sounded motherly and what in today's idiom would, I suppose, be called 'caring'.

About a mile away from the house the road stretched straight ahead to the brow of a hill. On the skyline a lone figure on horseback was trotting beside the road. As I drove closer I could make out that the rider was a woman. When I caught up with her I saw it was Annabel Silvester. She was moving smoothly along a grass verge to the right of the road. Astride a horse I thought she looked surprisingly elegant. Her legs and backside seemed to fit snugly into her jodhpurs. Her black hair, in non-equestrian mode usually slightly unkempt and matted, was netted neatly in a bun behind her head; it glistened like the morning dew. Her face was pink and healthy, though a slight frown appeared across her forehead when I slowed down the BMW alongside her and lowered my window. She seemed strangely concerned to see me.

'You're up early,' she shouted down at me.

I looked at my watch, which said seven-thirty. 'I know. I wanted to catch the first post from the village.'

This seemed to reassure her and I had the impression that she relaxed a little.

Just at that moment, as I was about to accelerate to pull ahead of her, we both heard it, faint at first and then deafeningly loud: the deep clatter of a helicopter shattering the morning stillness. Annabel's horse shied to the left and almost hit my car. She managed to rein him in tightly as the machine roared overhead.

'Michael Hildreth leaving for Norwich,' she shouted.

'For Norwich?'

'He's going to a wedding there; he said he would be back soon after lunch.'

'I see. I didn't know.' I felt strangely put out that she knew about Michael's movements and I didn't.

'See you at breakfast,' she said, and nudged the flanks of her black mare into a canter. Why, I wondered, was Annabel of all people mixed up with a crowd like the one staying at Greysham? For all her coarseness, I had always thought of her as a rather simple, honest person. I had known her for most of my life. She had sometimes been boisterous, occasionally rude, invariably loud, but never before had shown any signs of becoming a crook. I had placed her as being too well-bred and too tied up with her beloved horses.

Her mention of breakfast reminded me that I had intended to be first into the dining room; I wanted the opportunity to form my own impression of each of the guests as they came into the room. There would be nothing lost by viewing each one off guard before the fact of John's death became generally known. This plan had been only slightly modified by Michael's unexpected (for me, anyway) departure. I pressed my foot down on the accelerator; within seconds I was overtaking the now galloping Annabel.

As I approached the house, I saw Bobby Longfellow standing outside the front door. A cigar was sticking out of his mouth in Churchillian fashion. As I drove up behind him he was staring hard in the direction of the West Lawn from where Michael had presumably just taken off. I lowered the window of my car and shouted at him above the noise of the engine, 'Morning, Bobby. Good night's sleep?'

He turned round slowly to face me. His face was pale and blotchy and unfriendly. I thought he hesitated before he said, 'No, I never sleep at all in strange houses.'

'Not at all? How do you pass the night?'

'With the help of a little champagne and a good book,' he said. 'What about you, Jane? You look as frisky as ever. What have you been up to since we last met?'

I somehow didn't feel the question had been put from any genuine concern for my well-being. 'Sleeping and posting letters mainly,' I said simply, and drove my car to a corner of the forecourt, where I parked it.

Bobby's insomnia did not appear to have affected his appetite. When we entered the dining room together, he went straight over to the sideboard where, ignoring the several varieties of cereals, he helped himself to generous portions of fried food. Although we were alone in the room he effectively ignored me.

He deposited himself at one end of the long rectangular table, as far away as it was possible to be from where I sat, a glass of orange juice in front of me. He didn't say a word while he ate his eggs and bacon, not even to the pretty new housemaid, Fran, when she poured tea into a large cup beside him. Perhaps most strangely of all, he did not pick up any one of the morning papers which had been neatly laid out in rows on a side table.

I never knew a politician to be as apparently uninterested in news as Bobby was; not that he was badly informed – my impression was that he was, in fact, extremely knowledgeable about what was going on. I think he was just too interested in himself to care much about the written details of what others were up to. Another theory I had heard was that Bobby needed glasses to read and he was either too vain or too forgetful ever to have them with him. At any rate, the effect of all this was that his views on current events were usually rather original and very rarely repetitions of that day's *Times* leader, which is about as much as most of the MPs I know seem able to manage.

As no-one else had arrived yet, I decided to help myself to some toast. I went over to the sideboard and picked up a *Daily Mail* on the way back. I made a point of returning to my original seat with my back to the window and a good view of the main door to the room.

Eventually it turned out to be Richard Luke who was the next to arrive. He was dressed in grey slacks and a light blue polo neck sweater. His thin features were pale and his left eye twitched in a way that I had not noticed the night before.

'What a frightful din Michael made just now,' he said. 'I'd forgotten he was off to the Badstock wedding. I half thought of cadging a lift with him myself. I've known Jessica Badstock for years. With all the excitements last night I quite forgot to mention it to him.'

'Excitements?' I asked.

'All that nonsense John was going on about. Do you realise we only ate one course? You can't help feeling sorry for Mrs Briely. It must be a terrible disappointment when you've cooked a meal for however many people we are and none of it gets eaten. We only had a plate of smoked salmon.' He was labouring the point as if none of us had been there. 'No wonder I'm starving. I've never been to a dinner party before when we only ate one course.'

'And I've never been to one where the guests were accused of being murderers,' Bobby muttered. Then he returned to finishing the remains of his breakfast.

Richard now had his back to me as he helped himself to food from the sideboard so I couldn't catch the expression on his face as he asked, 'By the way, where is John? I thought this was to be the moment when he was to reveal all. You know the sort of thing: we all get lined up by Leyland and John tells us who dunnit. I'm quite looking forward to it.'

Neither Bobby nor I answered him. I was watching Bobby closely; having finished his meal he seemed to have gone into a trance. His eyes were focused on a silver salt cellar about a foot in front of him. Apparently unaffected by our lack of response, Richard sat himself down next to me.

'By the way,' he said, 'I've just seen Sylvia. She says she can't face breakfast and has gone for a walk. Anyone know what the plans are for today? I thought I might try to get in a round of golf at a course near Cirencester. I know the pro there. He'll give me a game if no one here wants to come with me.'

I had been concentrating on Richard while he had been speaking and so had failed to notice that Lucy Hildreth had glided silently into the room. There was a little more colour in her cheeks than there had been last night. I thought again how pretty she would be if she wasn't so sad-looking. She sat herself next to Bobby and in front of a fresh grapefruit. She was certainly the one person in the room who I thought might benefit from a good helping of fried food.

Richard started up again. 'What's everyone doing today? I don't want to be anti-social. If something's being organised I'm happy to tag along.'

'Better ask John,' Bobby advised. 'He's running our lives for the time being.'

'Where *is* John? Has anyone actually seen him this morning?' Richard seemed determined to press the question this time.

Bobby suddenly came to life; he glared at me with narrowed eyes. I felt he had been waiting for this moment since we had first entered the dining room together. He spoke very slowly. 'No, I haven't seen him. Have you, Jane? You've been up and about for longer than the rest of us. Do you know where he is?'

'Probably exercising Sambo.'

Sambo was John's favourite mare and the voice was Annabel's. She stood for a moment in the doorway slapping her riding crop against the palm of her hand. I couldn't help noticing again how attractive she looked in her tight riding breeches and well pressed white blouse. She had removed the net from the back of her head, allowing her long black hair to fall loosely down her neck. I thought I caught an admiring flicker in Bobby's eye, though I couldn't be sure. The main features of his face remained totally impassive. I wondered for a moment whether his expressionless gaze was a pose, some sort of mask to hide an inner fear. Did there exist anyone in the world who had succeeded in stripping that mask from him? I decided probably not. Bobby Longfellow was as he appeared: ruthless, selfish, unforgiving, coarse – and fascinating.

Giles Lester was the last house guest to arrive. When he did so he was strangely subdued. He was dressed in a thick tweed jacket, dark grey trousers and brown brogue shoes. Strands of his long brown hair hung lank down the side of his face.

He said nothing, not even 'good morning' as he helped himself to a bowl of corn flakes. He remained silent as he sat himself at the opposite end of the table from Bobby.

I looked at my watch. It was nearly nine o'clock. The time I had allotted myself was running out and I was making very poor progress.

'I think we should meet in the South Room at nine thirty,' I said.

'Why?' asked Bobby Longfellow.

'That'll give John his chance to tell us what's happening.'

'Why don't we just leave?' asked Richard.

'I wouldn't do that,' Lucy said quietly. 'He's got all the cards now.' She looked at me as if for reassurance, and I smiled at her.

Bobby Longfellow seemed to notice this interchange; he turned towards her and stared at her intently for a moment. She looked so young, almost in her teens: and yet I knew she was nearly thirty. Michael had married her just over eight years earlier.

Suddenly Bobby announced, 'OK, we'll meet in half an hour.' Then he pushed back his chair noisily, placed his napkin on the table and left the room with the abruptness we were becoming used to.

'I'll go and find Sylvia,' Annabel said. 'I think I know where she is.'

As I rose from my place, I noticed that Lucy remained motionless and apparently mystified by what was going on. When I passed her, her shoulder gave a twitch and I thought for a moment she was going to make a move to catch my arm. I paused beside her to give her the opportunity to make contact with me. Instead, her body seemed to go rigid and she turned her head away from me. There was no doubt about it, Lucy was a very strange lady; or at least she had become so in recent times. I wondered again what Michael saw in her. Perhaps it was the fact that she appeared so submissive and vulnerable. And yet it didn't seem to make sense that he should find her passivity exciting. Michael gave me the impression of needing to be stimulated and pampered. I didn't somehow see him getting his kicks from dominating poor little Lucy.

CHAPTER TEN

'Where the hell *is* John?' Richard Luke demanded, as the seven of us gathered together in the South Room. 'This weekend is beginning to get on my nerves.'

The clock on the mantelpiece showed nine forty. I decided it was safe to proceed.

'John's not coming,' I said.

'How do you know?' asked Sylvia.

'Because he's dead,' I said. My earlier conversation with the Office had indicated that they had no objection to John's death becoming known generally.

'How do you know?' This time the question was Bobby's.

'Because I found the body.'

I was watching their faces carefully. Extraordinarily there was no noticeable reaction from any of them. Each one stared at me with the same look of impassive hostility with which I had been greeted the day before.

'Well, I suppose that solves one problem,' Sylvia said. 'John can't make any more stupid accusations about people murdering other people, can he?'

I looked directly at her for a moment and then said, 'That's rather callous, isn't it?' I remembered John's words at dinner: 'We shall have to act fast before he kills again.' Or was it 'she'?

'Does Elizabeth know?' Richard asked. 'Does anyone know where Elizabeth is?'

'I know where she is,' Bobby said. Then looking straight at me he changed the subject.

'Where do you think this leaves things Jane?' he asked.

'Answer him,' Sylvia said. I must admit it came as a surprise to me that she should have taken some sort of lead in this discussion. I had always understood why Antonio should have found her physically attractive. She was very pretty indeed and never more so than today. She was wearing a beautifully designed deep pink dress. Her golden hair had been newly washed; her make-up had been skilfully and lightly applied. She simply glowed with beauty and good health. I had not, however, expected her to be the one to whom I would primarily need to address my remarks.

'It depends on how he was murdered and by whom,' I said.

'What Bobby meant is how much do you know about us?' Lucy asked. Surprising, too, that she had joined in.

'What I also meant,' Bobby added, 'is what business of Jane's is all this anyway?'

Bobby seemed determined to persist in referring to me in the third person in my presence.

'Where did you find the body?' Richard Luke asked from a seat in the far corner of the room by the window.

'At the bottom of the stairs.'

'So what happened to it?' he pressed.

'I moved it.'

'What on earth for?' asked Bobby.

Before I needed to answer there was a sudden sound of several cars pulling up outside the front door. I looked at my watch. The Office had done its job, although I wasn't getting very far with mine. This would be the Gloucestershire Police. Events were rapidly running out of my control.

'What the hell is going on?' Annabel asked.

'It'll be the police,' I said.

'Are you one of them?' Bobby asked.

'I think you can probably answer that for yourself.'

'What does that mean?' This time the question came from Richard.

'It means she's a member of the secret police and a threat to democracy,' Bobby said. 'From our point of view she's just a viper in our midst.'

'What's wrong with you, love?' Sylvia asked. 'Don't you get enough of it or something? With your money and good looks, Jane, you shouldn't have to mess around with the fuzz.' Sylvia seemed to be reverting to some long rejected way of speech.

I remember uncrossing my legs, leaning back on the sofa, and staring for a moment up to the ceiling. Where was all this getting me? To be honest, not very far. The only one of them who was definitely acting out of character was Giles Lester, who had not spoken a word all morning. Beyond that there was very little to go on. Longfellow, it was true, was being more directly rude to me than was necessary. Richard Luke was being sly, Sylvia Richards abrasive, Annabel quiet, and Lucy her usual peculiar self. None of this, of course, gave me much of a clue as to which one of them, if any, had murdered John.

Suddenly the door opened. A young superintendent in uniform came into the room. He was flustered.

'Which one's Lady Jane Hildreth?' he asked.

I stood up and faced him.

'Would you come outside a moment, ma'am?'

When we were in the hall, he said, 'I'm Superintendent Braithwaite. I am in charge of this job for the time being. The body's not where you told us it was.'

'What do you mean?'

'It's gone, if it ever was there. It's not in the cupboard under the stairs.'

'It's got to be here somewhere,' I insisted. 'Could I suggest you search the house from top to bottom?'

He gave me what he might have called 'one of those looks' and said, 'Ma'am, we've already started that.'

'Very good. Then I shall continue to pursue my enquiries in here,' I said, turning back to the door of the South Room.

'You do that, ma'am, and ask them to stay on when you're finished with them. We shall want to have a go ourselves – that's always assuming we don't find Lord Hildreth out riding somewhere. He won't be pleased at all if we have torn his beautiful house apart all for nothing. In that case, I shouldn't be surprised if the Chief Constable would have a few words to say to your boss, whoever he is. What are you, by the way? We couldn't figure out your outfit at all when we called them back this morning.'

I ignored the question and returned to the South Room. Bobby Longfellow was now sitting over by the window.

'Lost the body, have we?' he asked.

'How do you know?'

'By looking at your gorgeous face. It's gone white as chalk.'

I said, 'Everyone here must now be a suspect. The local CID and I will both need to talk to each of you individually.'

'You know what,' said Sylvia, who was lying full length on the sofa where I had previously been sitting 'I think you must be frigid. When all this is over, I'll give you a few lessons. That would be fun.' For the first time in the whole weekend, Bobby grinned.

'I'm afraid no-one may leave the house for the time being,' I said.

'On whose orders?' asked Bobby.

'Superintendent Braithwaite.' It was at that moment that I noticed that Annabel Silvester was crying. I decided to speak to her first.

CHAPTER ELEVEN

'Why were you so upset just now?' I asked Annabel when we were alone in the South Room. 'It's unlike you to show your feelings.' Tears were flooding into her eyes again.

'We've been such bloody fools,' she sobbed. 'I wish I could have my life all over again. All I ask for is to be left alone with my horses. Do you think we shall go to prison?'

'For what?'

'It was all done for Antonio.' She was weeping again.

'Shall we start at the beginning? How did you first meet Antonio? I think I know, but I would rather hear it in your own words.'

'I applied for a job with him as a groom. As you know, Jane, I had grown up with horses on our family farm in Somerset and I was pretty well trained to look after Antonio's polo ponies.' Her voice was deep and much firmer now. Her eyes were large and round and gave the impression of hidden strength.

'When did you first sleep with Antonio?' I asked. She screwed up her nose: a new and unexpected anger entered her eyes. I thought she was going to tell me to mind my own business. Instead, she said, 'About two years ago. It was his way of saying thank you to me for what I was doing for him – getting his drugs and things.'

'Did you love him?'
She nodded.
'Enough to kill him when he fell for another woman?'
She shook her head. 'Ours was never that kind of relationship, never exclusive. He always had plenty of other women around when I was with him. As long as I had my share of him, that was enough. If you like, I knew my place.'
'But all that changed when Elizabeth Hildreth came on the scene?' I asked. 'She wasn't some little Sylvia Richards, was she, who could be fitted in on Mondays to Thursdays? She demanded Antonio's total commitment and he gave it to her?'
Annabel nodded and sniffed.
'That put your relationship on rather a different footing, didn't it?'
'Yes. I didn't see much of him once Elizabeth came into the picture.'
'So what did you do about it?'
She hesitated for an instant and from that moment I knew I would have to discount most of her further answers. In any case, she had lost track.
'What did you say?' she asked.
'What was your response when Elizabeth came into the picture?'
'To get frustrated and blood angry, I suppose.'
'You continued to ferry drugs for him?'
'Yes. I went all over the world.'
'Knowing the risk and knowing also that your friendship with Antonio was from his point of view virtually at an end?'
She was silent.
'Did he blackmail you to make you carry on?'
This question seemed to trigger some deep emotion within her. Her face became very red. She was angry. 'No more bloody questions. You've had your lot. From

now onwards we will deal through lawyers.'

There were one or two more questions I still badly needed to put to her. I had to try to find some way of getting through to her again.

'Don't you see,' I pleaded, 'I couldn't give a damn myself about what you did for Antonio with drugs. My concern is with how he died and, possibly more importantly, how John Hildreth was murdered. If Antonio was blackmailing you to run drugs for him, you must remain on the suspect list.'

'I can't help you any further,' she said and our conversation was at an end.

My next interview was with Sylvia Richards, who in her tarty little way gave me almost exactly the same story as Annabel's. Again, she had been jilted by Antonio with the arrival of Elizabeth Hildreth. Once more, there was the implication of blackmail in order to make her continue to run errands for him.

'Said he could arrange to have me shopped if I gave up on him, so I just carried on.' Sylvia did, however, confirm what I had already suspected and what I had fervently hoped would be the case, that Michael Hildreth was no part of the drugs caper that she had been tied up with. In fact, this weekend was the first time she had ever clapped eyes on him. 'More's the pity. He's quite a hunk, don't you think?'

Richard Luke, Bobby Longfellow and Giles Lester were, however, very good friends of hers and had been a great source of comfort to her when Antonio had 'gone funny'.

'You would describe his behaviour in the end as funny, would you?' I asked.

'No, I wouldn't, but it's the politest word I can think of at the moment. If I knew you better I might describe it rather differently.'

Lucy Hildreth's response to my questioning was rather surprising. She seemed suddenly, at least for this occasion, to have joined the real world, and came close even to giving an impression of enjoying the whole proceedings. Her little snub nose twitched before she answered my questions; at one moment she even smiled, showing a straight line of beautifully white teeth. I tried to exploit the opportunity by smiling back, and she immediately leant forward and gave me a piercing look from behind the long brown hair which, with her sudden movement, had fallen across her face like a curtain. There were depths to Lucy's character which I imagined Michael had explored and found exciting.

As it turned out, however, I didn't get much out of her. She did offer the rather gratuitous information that she and Michael were not part of any general conspiracy to trade drugs. I had not suggested that they were. She seemed to want to emphasise the point, saying that she had been a user from time to time but not a dealer. I asked her how well she had known Antonio. She seemed surprised by the question – almost shocked. There was certainly a pause before she answered.

'I hardly knew him at all, poor man.'

'Poor man? You felt sorry for him, although you hardly knew him?'

'He was murdered, wasn't he? That was terrible.' She must have sensed that I was taking a particular interest in this remark, because suddenly she wanted to retract it. She rubbed her forehead with the back of her hand and said, 'It's nothing. It doesn't matter.'

But I was all the keener to go on with it.

'How can you say that Antonio was murdered, Lucy? John could well have been mistaken, you know. No one has ever shown that Antonio took the heroin with his drink against his will or that the combined effect caused his fall from the pony. You have to show both even to have a case for murder. You would have in particular to show that death had occurred from some sort of respiratory failure.'

'John mistaken?' She opened her mouth wide. Her dark watery eyes looked startled. She shrugged. 'It's what everyone has been saying, isn't it?' And then, quite unexpectedly, she began to cry. Large tears rolled silently and slowly down her white face.

'What's wrong, Lucy?' I asked. 'You're not very happy these days, are you?'

At this the tears stopped as abruptly as they had begun.

'I don't like being asked silly questions,' she said in a voice which was much deeper and harsher than I had ever heard it before. Her extraordinarily rapid change of mood worried me.

'OK, Lucy, let's call it a day; but if you ever need me, you know where I can be reached, don't you? You've got all my home numbers. You can always leave a message on any of my answering machines if I'm out.'

She nodded absently and got up to leave.

I was now left with the three male house guests, whom I had purposely kept waiting. Before I called each one of them in, I felt I had to remind myself about the objective of my enquiries. This was not, in essence, to find out who killed John Hildreth, let alone to decide on whether or not Antonio had been murdered. All that was the job of the police. My task was a very straightforward one. It was merely to try to establish whether there was any connection between the fact of the two deaths and John's hints about a threat to national security. This was the limit of the Office's interest in the matter. It was as well to remind myself that I was not there as some kind of private sleuth, nor as a busybody who had a rather clear personal interest in bringing things to a conclusion.

In the event, my interviews with Longfellow, Luke and Lester were very short. They had collectively decided not to cooperate with me at all. Inevitably, Bobby Longfellow was their spokesman. (Giles Lester seemed to have gone almost dumb and was incapable of using words of more than one syllable).

'The trouble is, Jane,' Bobby told me, 'we think you are extremely pretty. Some of us would have liked very much to have gone to bed with you, but we don't trust you, and do you know why? We think it's quite probable that you're up to your neck in John's death yourself – assuming that John is indeed dead, and no one except for you seems at all certain that he is.

'If it turns out that he has been murdered, we think it quite possible that you did it, God knows why. Perhaps he was upsetting your department in some way. I tell you one thing – if this is the way the British KGB works, there are going to be one hell of a lot of questions asked about it in the House of Commons. In the meantime, my dear Jane, it's no dice. You're wasting your time with us. We'll give any help we can, which will be practically nil, to the police, but not to you.'

As I crossed the hall from the drawing room after this confrontation with Bobby, I was met by Superintendent Braithwaite.

'The good news,' he said, 'is that your suitcase was left behind in the cupboard and is now safely back in your room. The bad news is that there is no sign of his Lordship. We've been all over the house and I shall have to start calling some of my men off this job soon. They're needed for football work at Bristol. Avon and Somerset are a bit short and have asked for our help this afternoon. Two of my sergeants and I will start interviewing the staff and your house guest friends. Is the plan for them to stay another night here?'

'I would like that,' I said.

'Is it wise, I ask myself?' he mocked. 'What with all these murders going on.'

'Look, Superintendent, until you find Lord Hildreth, who witnesses will tell you was hale and hearty and very much around until eleven thirty last night, I don't think your sarcasm is quite fair.'

'You're right, ma'am. I'm sorry. I appreciate you have your job to do; perhaps one day you'll accept a drink off me and tell me exactly what it is.'

Now that he had become more likeable I felt I could begin to ask favours from him. 'If we do all stay for one more night,' I said, 'I think we could do with the odd constable giving us a bit of cover in the small hours.'

'We'll certainly do our best,' he said.

'Oh, and there's one other thing,' I added. 'Michael Hildreth, who I believe to be the new Lord Hildreth, will be back in his helicopter around about three o'clock. He went to a wedding in Norwich.'

'God Almighty,' said the policeman. 'Is this how they all live? By the way, your name's Hildreth too, isn't it?'

CHAPTER TWELVE

I don't know whether I was first to hear the helicopter. I was certainly the only person to go out to meet it.

The house guests had finished lunch and coffee was being served in silence by Leyland in the South Room. We had tacitly agreed to keep off all sensitive subjects, so conversation had been limited to a brief reference to the news (football hooliganism) and to the weather (it was the first bright day for over a month). Superintendent Braithwaite had persuaded everyone to delay departure until Sunday morning so that his men would not have to rush the interviews. Richard Luke, always cautious, had asked whether it would be advisable to have his lawyer join him from London for the interviews. The Superintendent looked at him for a moment and said, 'Not unless you have something to hide. It'll all be very routine stuff.'

'All right for us to leave the estate for a few hours?' asked Bobby.

'Why not?' answered the policeman. 'You're not under arrest. We haven't even established that there has been a crime yet; its going to be difficult to do so until we find Hildreth. But I would be grateful if you would refrain from speaking to the press. I would rather find his Lordship first before the vultures step in on me. But that's probably asking too much. They've got nostrils like radio beacons, those boys.

Some of them will sniff out a story before it's happened and they won't necessarily be imagining it, either.'

'Always believe everything you read in the press,' Bobby muttered. 'It's as sound a rule as any.'

'I think I'll have that game of golf,' Richard said. 'Anyone remember what time Leyland said we had to be on parade for dinner?'

'He didn't,' said Annabel. 'He's gone completely off colour today. I can't get any sense out of him at all. It's all very odd. Do you think he's the one who's bunked off with poor old John's body?'

There was a shout from Lucy. 'What a stupid and horrid idea,' she said and rushed out of the room with her hair and her long cotton skirt flowing out behind her.

The suddenness of her departure left everyone a little stunned. Like the rest of the party, I stared in the direction of the door which she had slammed behind her and I thought hard about her behaviour. I felt there had to be a pattern to it. Her sensitivity to the mention of Leyland was especially interesting. I wondered whether it tied in at all with the very special attention he had paid to her the previous evening.

'Now you've upset Lucy,' Bobby said. 'You must admit, Annabel, it was a rather silly remark. We don't even know John's dead yet. I, for one, certainly don't intend to take young Jane's word for it.'

Bobby's faith in me clearly wasn't growing as the weekend proceeded. Nor was his appetite diminishing. At lunch he returned to the sideboard three times for more helpings of cold pheasant.

'I wonder if Lucy knows something about Leyland that we don't,' Richard Luke said.

'Leave Mr Leyland to me, if you don't mind, ladies and gents,' Superintendent Braithwaite intervened firmly.

It was not immediately clear at whose invitation the policeman had joined the company for lunch. His presence had certainly not added to the conviviality of the occasion. The hostility towards him seemed to go deeper than an understandable resentment caused by the fact that everyone there was under his suspicion.

Bobby seemed to express the general distaste for Braithwaite when he asked with his customary rudeness, 'Why do we have a Superintendent on this job? In books it's always inspectors.'

'It's like everything else these days: too many chiefs not enough Indians,' Richard answered.

'With the taxpayer footing the bill, of course,' Bobby added for good measure.

I thought both he and Richard were being a little foolhardy. It was certainly on the cards that Superintendent Braithwaite would find some opportunity to have his own back on them.

I had to admit, however, that the atmosphere seemed to have eased considerably since breakfast that morning. I wondered for a brief moment whether it was possible that some specific event had occurred, known to the rest of the group but unreported to me, which had reduced the tension noticeably. Only Giles Lester seemed to be missing the new mood. After lunch, he took a seat on the fireguard and sat staring moodily at the crackling logs. He had still not spoken a single word in my hearing since going to bed the previous night. Part of me rather hoped he would remain that way. A state of gloomy silence rather suited him. It made him appear almost tragic; but it was also so unnatural as to be a little sinister. I could not help pondering once more the question of what could possibly have upset him with such apparently traumatic effect.

After I had finished my coffee, I decided to wander into the garden. I needed to be alone for a while, away from the general nastiness of the other houseguests. I sat on a bench at the back of the house facing west across well-cut and gently sloping lawns. I lay back and felt the warm rays of the autumn sun on my face. It had been a busy summer. During its passage I had travelled to many places, including Australia, Hawaii, and Hong Kong. There had been adventures and sadness and fun and some danger, but there had been very little time to think. It was probably just as well that a woman of my age with no family, no children, no husband, should not meditate too hard about where life was taking her.

There was, of course, a price to be paid for living for one's job. I knew I was tired and so more vulnerable, physically and emotionally, than I should be. I had promised myself a holiday on several recent occasions. It was always going to be something active; not for me lying on a beach for very long, roasting myself gradually like a kebab for the man of the moment. I might have been prepared to go on a sherry-drinking binge round the Spanish fiestas; I had acquired a bit of a taste for flamenco dancing. But what I really wanted to do was to spend a few weeks in India photographing the brilliant colours and trying to capture the frenetic movement of human life there; or, failing that, to go skiing somewhere high up, using helicopters for the ascent. Every time I was about to get around to doing something about it, another job had come up. There had certainly been no shortage of action that year, but there had been a price to pay – I was tired; I no longer fully trusted my reflexes. For someone in my business, that's not good.

I closed my eyes and tried to loosen my limbs. This weekend, I knew, was taking its own special toll. Hardened though I was to violence, it would take some time to recover from the events of the past few hours. What on earth could have happened to poor

John? It may seem macabre to say so, but he had looked somehow attractive in death. I had suddenly felt his loss in a way I had not experienced for many years. I wondered for the first time whether we might have made it in our marriage if I had been more forceful, more determined perhaps to make it work. I told myself that it would have been impossible. It was not in my character to dominate a man. I was decisive and forceful enough in my work, but that was different. I had to be. My speed of reaction had saved my life on more than one occasion. But in my relations with men I knew I was weak and responsive and vacillating.

Perhaps in this case my looks and my wealth had acted against me. Perhaps they had made life too easy. I had never really been forced to make choices. It was not that I was promiscuous; or at least, I have never seen myself in that way – that is to say, I am usually very much in control of my physical and emotional senses. It is more that I have been able to take what I have wanted until I have had enough. Very rarely has it been a case of either or; even more rarely of being denied what I have wanted. There is something else: I am a perfectionist, certainly in my job but also in what I look for in a man. My problem, I suppose, is that I am a romantic who never finds the perfect man. So I pick and choose the good bits from a wide range. In this way I piece together a cerebral identikit fit of the perfect bloke. It is my good fortune, I suppose, that without my having to take any positive action, the romance is always conducted on my terms.

I stretched my legs and wondered whether it would be forever so. As I grew older, would I be compelled to make more exacting choices? Would the choice even be left to me? Perhaps in the future men would not respond when I twirled my skirt or looked them straight in the eye. Perhaps their coolness would no longer be caused simply by nervousness or jealousy. Perhaps there would be those who quite simply would not find me particularly desirable. Now I thought of it, John Hildreth had been the only man in life to have discarded me.

It has to be said that my lifestyle didn't make for continuity in my relationships with men. Above all, romance, if that is the right word for it, wasn't allowed to interfere with my job. An affair has even been known to have been the cause of the successful completion of an assignment. I cannot even deny that I did not will it that way.

Perhaps I had become too rational, too objective, too ruthless. Perhaps I should let my hair down and abandon myself, before it was too late.

My thoughts were disrupted by the distant drone of an approaching helicopter. Subconsciously I must have been listening for it, waiting for this moment. Its anticipation must, I suppose, have been the main reason why I had left the stifling atmosphere of the South Room and why my thoughts had drifted to my relationships with men. I wanted to be the first to meet him, to tell him all I knew, before he had the opportunity to have his mind twisted by Bobby Longfellow and his chums, or before Superintendent Braithwaite could intervene with his pen-sucking and his form-filling.

Despite all that I have said, Michael Hildreth was the one man who both fascinated and frightened me a little. He was so full of paradoxes: physically strong, courageous – especially on the polo field – financially brilliant, and yet, in a strange way, unsure of himself, the eternal younger brother, married for eight years to the pathetic little Lucy. My mind wandered back yet again to the question of what he saw in her. It certainly wasn't her fertility: Michael and Lucy had no children.

There must be some mysterious power hidden in those vacant sorrowful eyes. I had never seen him be unkind to her, and yet I have to say that in my presence he had never demonstrated any real love for her; but there again, I suspected that Michael was not very demonstrative at the best of times.

And now he was about to pilot his helicopter onto the west lawn. Though he did not yet know it, he was on the point of inheriting great estates and titles. In the past few hours he had, in fact, become one of the richest men in the world.

The aircraft flew into sight from behind a copse lining a hill to my right. Rapidly reducing its altitude, it came in a straight line towards me. It appeared for a moment that the pilot was aiming directly at the house. I could not believe what I was seeing; I was about to witness a terrible accident. Then, seconds before the point of collision, the machine banked at almost a ninety degree angle and skimmed a few feet over where I was standing.

I could see the smile on Michael's face. He seemed to be piloting with one hand. His left thumb was pointing upwards and his fist pushed towards me in some sort of salute. This was the man I had once heard recite one of his own poems in a café in Chelsea. I remembered the tears flowing down his cheeks as he did so.

The helicopter landed about a hundred yards away from me. As the blades came to a rest the pilot, dressed in a khaki flak jacket and grey trousers, jumped from the cockpit, his long hair blown behind him by the airstream. I remembered what had been said about his cruelty. A girl friend of mine had once seen him shoot one of his own polo ponies dead, ostensibly because it had fallen and broken a leg but in reality, according to her, because the pony had let him down in a practice game.

Michael unzipped his jacket, pushed his hands

deep into the pockets and produced a large cigar. Under his left arm he carried a black top hat. I began to walk towards him. He perched the hat precariously over his forehead and grinned. I realised I hadn't really thought out how best to break the news of his brother's death to him. His present behaviour was going to make this even more difficult. As I came nearer to him I saw he was wearing his morning suit under the army-style jacket. His red braces showed beneath an open waistcoat. The whole effect was slightly bizarre. When he was near enough, he put his cigar in his mouth and shouted at me through clenched teeth: 'Hello, Jane. What have I done wrong now?'

It was hard to tell whether he was irritated or pleased to see me.

'I've got bad news, Michael. I thought I should be the first to tell you.'

'Very kind, very kind.' He was still just too far away from me to catch my mood.

'John's dead.'

'John's dead, is he?' The ridicule in his question meant that I was still not getting through to him. His mind hadn't focused properly on what I was saying. I had a sense for the first time that he was distracted by my presence. He was staring not so much at my face as at my figure, at the flare in my dress, at my legs and my hair, which had been blown by the slipstream of the helicopter. What he saw seemed to give him pleasure.

Nor can I claim that I objected to this attention. Part of me, possibly a large part of me, greatly enjoyed it. If I am being totally honest, I wanted to hold it. For a moment each of us seemed to have the other in some sort of a spell. In the end it was I who broke it.

'Murdered.' I spoke the word slowly so that he would not misunderstand it. Even so, he seemed to hesitate. His reaction was not immediate. Then he looked at me suspiciously. His grin faded. 'How do you know?'

'I saw the body.'

'Oh, Christ,' he said. 'Have you been on the bottle or something?'

'You know that's unlikely. It must be very hard for you to take it in, Michael. John's dead.'

He looked straight down at me. His eyes were suddenly glazed and bloodshot. For a moment he said nothing. His face was drained. His cheeks seemed to have deflated. I have never seen a man's face collapse so fast; suddenly he looked gaunt and haggard. It was almost as if he had been preparing himself for the news for some time. It was a strange reaction, something different from grief. I stored the impression in my mind without being able to define it properly at the time.

Wearily and as if making a great effort he almost whispered. 'Where is the body? I must go and see him.'

'The body is missing.' My responses were becoming automatic.

'Missing? What on earth's going on here, Jane? What are you people up to?' His questions were becoming mechanical, almost awkward. The anger had turned synthetic; it was as if he was embarrassed to enquire further. Suddenly he had associated me with authority. I began to feel that I might have been wrong to come out to tell him myself about his brother's death.

'I can't tell you any more,' I said. 'We don't know.'

'We?'

'The police. They're doing their best.' It was all beginning to sound very weak.

'I should think they bloody well are. Where is everybody, anyway?'

'Lucy, you mean?' This time it was his turn to look

mystified. He paused for a moment and then mumbled in a way that made it hard to hear him. 'Yes, that's right, Lucy. Where's Lucy?'

'I think she went up to her room.'

'Is Leyland with her?'

'I don't know. Should he be?' It was clearly becoming of some importance to understand more about the relationship between Lucy Hildreth and the family butler. Michael ignored my question.

'And the others?' he asked. 'Where are the others? Bobby and Richard and Annabel and Sylvia.'

'I think most of them are still in the house.' He seemed relieved. I thought he relaxed a little.

'And you, Jane? What are you up to? On the job, eh?'

I wondered how much he really knew about me. I decided not to reply. At any rate the effect of his having asked the question was to calm him down completely. Suddenly he was totally composed, at least on the surface.

'So what's the form now?' he asked, in a tone which I can only describe as now being strangely 'matter of fact'.

I tried my best to match his mood and to sound as practical and as rational as I could. 'There's not much we can do until we find the body.'

We began to walk side by side towards the house. When we reached the bench that I had left a few minutes before, he turned to me. 'Let's sit down for a moment – give me time to collect my thoughts.'

He spoke gently but it was a command. Even had I wished to do so, there would have been no question of disobeying him. We lowered ourselves onto the seat together, synchronised, in tandem, as if we were dancing or making love. His next words showed, however, that his concentration was elsewhere.

'I think I heard you say you had seen the body. Was that right?'

'Perhaps it would be best if I told you the whole story.'

I began at the point at which the house party had broken up during dinner the previous evening and ended with the scene in the South Room just before I had left to meet him here. I told him almost all I knew. With the exception of one item, there was very little I felt I needed to hold back from him. I tried in particular to recapture for him my feelings for John when I found him dead at the foot of the stairs.

As I spoke I didn't feel Michael was listening to me very carefully. In fact, there were moments when I sensed I had lost his attention altogether. At the time I put this lack of concentration down to his shock and distress.

When I had finished he simply said, 'God almighty, what happens now?' It occurred to me that he had been the only person that day apparently to have taken what I had told him on trust. It gave me the first genuinely warm feeling I had experienced since coming back to Greysham. I forgot his question and focused my mind on Michael himself. He seemed to sense my mood: quite unexpectedly he took hold of my hand and looked straight into my eyes. His grip was firm and pleasurable.

'Thanks, Jane. It was very good of you to come out to meet me and to tell me all this yourself.' Then, without warning, the moment passed. The mood changed once more; he dropped my hand.

'Which one of them did it, do you think? There are not many to choose from, for Christ's sake. You must have some ideas. That's what you're paid for, isn't it?'

I reacted to this instinctively and in kind. I had no reason to allow myself to be bullied by Michael, not yet anyway.

'I was invited as a guest for a quiet weekend,' I said. 'I'm meant to be here on holiday. What's more I'm not a policewoman; and please try to remember I'm not on the Hildreth payroll these days.' As a statement of fact this last point was not quite true, but my anger seemed to have the right effect. He became nice again.

'Do you think John's death ties in with the Antonio business?' He didn't wait for my answer. 'My God, suppose John was right. What a mess. What a bloody mess.'

He stretched his legs out onto the grass. His calf leather dress boots covered his ankles. He opened his mouth wide and yawned. 'So I'm going to be Lord Hildreth: Lord bloody Michael Hildreth. There are going to be one or two changes around here, I'll tell you that for free, Jane. Decent shooting parties for a start. John wouldn't have more than half a dozen guns at a time. Never could make that out. Poor old John, what do you think he was rabbiting on about last night? I know Bobby and his chums; there's nothing fundamentally wrong with them. John was onto something, but he didn't have it quite right. I'd put a lot of money on that.' He shook his head. 'Lord Michael Hildreth: yes, your Lordship; no, your Lordship; will your Lordship be taking his seat in the House of Lords? Your Lordship's brother never did. I doubt it, Leyland. I never was much good at making speeches. I leave that to great men like Mr Longfellow; women and horses are more my thing.'

I wasn't sure whether all this was being put on for my benefit or whether he was simply going through some sort of mental self-adjustment process.

'What about her Ladyship?' I asked.

'Who?'

'Lucy.'

He turned to me. There was a wild cruel streak in his eyes. He tossed his head like a highly strung mare.

'Lucy's all right,' he said. 'Did you hear what I said, Jane? She's OK.'

I was no psychiatrist, but it was not hard to diagnose his barely suppressed hysteria. This, it seemed to me, was only indirectly related, if at all, to the death of his brother, John. I began to think even harder than before about Lucy Hildreth.

CHAPTER THIRTEEN

I thought a lot about my meeting with Michael as I lay in bed that night. His reaction to the news of his brother's death had been very odd. It had been not so much one of shock as of suppressed anger. This had made it all the more strange that neither he nor Lucy had been present at dinner that night. The other absentee had been Leyland who had had himself replaced by one of the girls from the village. Margaret, I think her name was. She managed to smash one plate and spill gravy from the roast duck down my satin evening dress.

Richard Luke had been right: it *was* 'spooky' lying in bed in a house knowing that John's killer was probably only a few yards away. We had lingered in the drawing room over coffee and brandy. No one had seemed very willing to break from the comfort and protection of the crowd. At last, well past midnight, we had reluctantly said goodnight to each other and climbed up the stairs, which for me had such unpleasant memories. Not even the presence of a local bobby by the front door, graciously laid on by my new friend Braithwaite, had been totally reassuring.

I must have dozed off to sleep sometime between one and two in the morning, because I woke with a start when I sensed that I was not alone in my room. I tried to focus my eyes into the gloom. A shadowy human figure moved across the end of my bed; then another. I couldn't make out their faces and realised they must be wearing hoods that covered their heads completely.

I suppose that subconsciously I had been expecting something like this to happen. I dug my fingernails into the palms of my hands to make sure that I was fully awake, then I threw back my sheets and kicked hard at the figure in front. I missed his groin and hit him in the shins; there was a grunt of pain. I rolled sharply to my left. Immediately they both jumped on top of me and one of them pinned my arms above my head.

We must have remained in this position for several seconds, all of us breathing heavily, no one saying a word. Then I was pulled to a sitting position and my arms were forced painfully behind my back. One of the intruders tossed a sort of boiler suit towards me. Still no one spoke. I decided this was not the moment to offer more resistance.

'If you want me to put this thing on, you'll have to let go of my arms,' I said.

My right arm was released. I got off the bed and began to struggle to pull the suit over my nightie, with my left hand still held firmly behind my back, and balancing in the dark, first on one foot, then on the other. It couldn't have been a very elegant performance. An uncomfortable bulge formed itself inside the top of the trouser section. Despite this, I managed somehow to zip up the jacket part. As I did so, one of them handed me a pair of blackened tennis shoes, which fitted me exactly.

I was just beginning to appreciate how well planned the operation had been when I noticed the rope tied to a central heating pipe. I saw that this trailed over the windowsill and into the blackness outside, presumably down into the courtyard. Before I had time fully to consider its implications, one of them grabbed the rope's end and swung himself across the ledge; the other held my arms firmly behind my back and pushed me forward.

The prospect of following the figure in front of me out of the window did not of itself cause me any alarm. I have been well trained in the art of climbing down ropes in the dark. I once had to descend a hundred-foot cliff in a thunderstorm with a missile launcher on my back. No, I wasn't nervous as I swung my right leg out of the window, I was puzzled.

If they wanted to kill me, why hadn't they done so while I had been lying in bed? They had certainly had ample opportunity. Perhaps they were simply taking me to a more convenient spot to assassinate me there. I remembered the strange positioning of John's body at the bottom of the stairs. Had they made him walk to his own execution? Willingly or, as I was now, with force?

There were a lot of questions. I began to wonder now whether I would ever get around to getting any answers for them. Immediate death in the woods outside was one prospect which lay before me; it was more likely, though, that they were preserving me for something more creative; otherwise why all the fancy planning – the shoes which fitted exactly and all the rest of the preparations?

I began to approach the ground and could see the figure who had gone in front of me prepare for my arrival. For a moment he seemed to crouch, coiled like a snake. The whites of his eyes shone out of the two slits in the balaclava. Then, as soon as I was within his reach, before my feet had touched the earth – before, that is, I had a chance to gain some sort of balance, he leapt at me with considerable force. I landed hard on my stomach with his weight on my back.

I have to admit my captor had taken a wise

precaution; had he allowed me to make contact with the ground, I would undoubtedly have given him a very hard kick, this time making sure to incapacitate him. I would have then been in a rather better position to receive his partner, who was now silhouetted on the window ledge above me. As it was, handcuffs were locked around my wrists and a blindfold was tied over my eyes, while I lay flat out on the wet earth, my mouth full of sodden moss. I remember to this day its bitter taste.

The wind had dropped and with my eyes blindfolded my hearing grew more acute. I distinctly heard the thud of the rope as it fell somewhere near me; then there was a slight thud, which sounded like the rubber-soled feet of the man from the windowsill hitting the ground. Presumably he had managed to get down without the aid of the rope: not too difficult given the height and doubtless the existence of countless ledges and the odd drainpipe. I imagined he must have thrown the rope ahead of him. I couldn't help but be impressed again by the slickness of the whole operation. Someone had given my capture a great deal of thought.

After a few minutes of total silence, I heard the scraping of feet and then a distant whistle. This was apparently the signal for action. I was lifted to my feet and pushed forward. Still no one spoke, though I could hear their breathing.

When we had walked for a few yards, I was halted and made to turn round in circles several times. Thus disorientated, I was marched in what appeared to be a straight line. The surface beneath my feet was hard and I assumed we were walking on the drive or across one of the courtyards. In any case, we did not go far before I heard the click of a door unlocking and the slight squeak as it opened. I was lifted sharply up by my feet and elbows. We appeared to be going down some steps. In the distance someone coughed. The noise echoed. Then my feet were placed on the ground and I was standing again. There was a scraping sound behind me and I was pulled down onto a chair. The muffled steps of my captors receded.

I sat in complete silence for about half an hour. Then, once more, I could hear the soft approach of deadened footsteps. Somebody was sitting close beside me. I could hear his breathing. His breath was heavy and unhealthy; it smelt of red wine.

'Listen very carefully, Jane,' he whispered. I tried desperately to recognise the voice, but I couldn't penetrate the disguise of the whisper. 'In a moment we are going to remove the gag from your mouth. Our conversation is likely to be much more constructive – and, dare I say, mutually beneficial if, like me, you speak in a whisper. Before freeing you to talk, let me, however, give you an idea as to the subject matter. My friends and I want to know what you have done with Lord Hildreth. My friends and I doubt that he is dead. We do know, however, that he had connections with British Intelligence, as indeed, of course, you do. We know also that he had begun to form some theories about the operations of my colleagues and me. Not surprisingly, we would like to talk over this knowledge with him.'

I still had no firm confirmation of whether or not John had worked for the Office. What I did know was that he was dead. It occurred to me that my best course of action now was to persuade my inquisitor of this fact, but to leave him with the impression that I and others had picked up where John had left off. Clearly my job was to try to find out precisely where in the minds of my captors that had been.

'Nod your head if you would like to enter into conversation on the terms I have outlined,' the voice whispered. 'We will need to use force on you if you make a noise.' I nodded. Hands began to untie a knot at the back of my head.

When I was free to speak, but not to see, I whispered into the darkness, 'What I first have to do is to find a way of persuading you that John is dead. This is going to be hard, because for the moment there is no body to show you. Bear in mind, perhaps, that he was at one time my husband. I loved him very much. For me to invent the details of the way I found his body would be, to say the least, unnatural.'

I then went over the events of the previous night as accurately as possible. When I had finished there was silence, broken only by the now faint breathing beside me. I assumed that it was the same man sitting there, more by the winey smell of his breath than by any sound he made. In the distance, or may be it was quite close – when you can't see you have a false idea of space – something metallic was dropped. Again, I was conscious of the echo. It occurred to me that we might be in the chapel.

'I don't necessarily believe you, but we must assume that Hildreth told you most of what he knew and that you have already passed this up the line.'

'You may be right,' I said.

The whisper, which had been aggressive and self-confident, now became more conciliatory.

'The question is whether it is possible for us to come to some arrangement.' The voice was still disguised but I was sure I was beginning to recognise some of its mannerisms. There was an edge to the words, almost a sneer, which was somehow familiar.

'That depends both on what you have to offer and on what you want from us.' An early part of my training had been to learn how to freewheel like this when the occasion demanded it.

'The purpose of this charade,' the voice said, 'is to ask you quite specifically whether you have been given permission to deal with us. I am sure you understand it is impossible for us to speak openly with you until we are clear what attitude your masters are taking towards us.'

'I have already indicated this depends on exactly what it is that you want from them.'

'I think you already know the answer: a chance to talk to them and the right to go on living outside gaol.'

'The first part shouldn't be too hard to arrange,' I said.

'You must do better than that, Jane, before we will agree to talk properly; surely Hildreth made that clear?'

There was a new urgency to his question.

'He certainly did,' I lied, 'but there is no way I can offer you a free pardon at this stage. You must know that. If you still want to bargain, I suggest we do just that and see what comes of it. The alternative is that we catch up with you anyway.'

'And in the process let you know exactly who we are for free?'

'That's inevitable, I'm afraid; we certainly can't go on meeting like this, not if I have anything to do with it.'

For a moment there was a pause; he seemed to be working out how to proceed from here. Then he said: 'If this goes wrong, it could be very dangerous; I'm not just thinking about you, Jane. Many people could get hurt.'

'I can't speak for the others,' I said, 'but I'm happy to try to look after myself. What's more, if necessary, there is a whole department of people behind me to pick up where I leave off.'

There was another long silence, which must have lasted the best part of a minute. Then he said, 'I think we have to talk to you again.'

'When?' I asked.

'Very soon. I shall have to speak to my friends but I think late this evening might do nicely.'

'Where?'

'Your cottage at Chipping Campden.'

He either knew me personally very well or had made a careful study of me. (For reasons of security, knowledge of my cottage in the Cotswolds was fairly restricted though, naturally, it was by no means a total secret). I had no intention, however, of showing that I had become genuinely intrigued by the turn in the conversation.

'Wouldn't that be a little risky for you?' I asked. 'I might have protection.'

'We'll be able to look after ourselves, don't you worry. In any case, when you hear what we have to tell you, you won't need protection.'

'Will you be masked?'

'No, we shall come as ourselves.'

'I will recognise you, won't I?'

'Not all of us.'

'What about you, Mr Mysteryman? I have a funny feeling I know you, possibly rather well?'

'That, dear lady, you will find out later. Please be ready to meet us at six o'clock. Now I am going to arrange for you to be taken back to your room. Needless to say, it would be most helpful from all our points of view if you were not to discuss this conversation with any of the house guests. As for communicating with your office, the more you do that the better. All I would ask of you is to encourage them not to jump to premature conclusions. They are very good at that, your people. Nor should they react too quickly. We have goods to offer and so, you will find, have you. Each of us could also spoil the bargain. I hope it will not be your people, Lady Hildreth. I hope so very much.'

After this I was led back to the wall of the house at

the foot of my bedroom window. When they took off my blindfold, the two figures beside me in balaclavas seemed to be the same ones who had abducted me.

'Will you need any further help?' one of them asked me in a whisper that had a French lilt.

I looked up at the window, noticed the drainpipe and two small ledges.

'No, I'll be all right,' I said.

'OK, we'll see you later,' the other man whispered. He spoke with a rather high-pitched American accent.

CHAPTER FOURTEEN

No one said much at breakfast the next day, though Giles Lester opened his mouth for the first time in twenty-four hours to ask when the police were coming. Everyone looked at me. Not knowing the answer, I shrugged.

'Braithwaite is sending one of his people in for an hour or so around ten o'clock, just to recheck one or two points. Then we can all go home. As it's Sunday, he doesn't want too many people working overtime,' Richard Luke quietly informed us.

'How do you know?' Sylvia Richards asked. For once she looked tired. She had tried to disguise the pallor of her face with heavy make-up. This merely had the effect of making her look tatty.

Richard glanced at her with, I thought, disapproval. 'I asked him,' he said.

'What a blessing. I can't wait to leave.' Annabel Silvester broke what seemed to be a growing tension. Some of the sparkle had returned to her eyes. Her hair was windswept and her cheeks flushed. Her athletic body was buttoned tightly into a pair of light blue jeans and a matching canvas jacket. She had evidently been riding already.

Michael and Lucy Hildreth did not appear at breakfast. It was the second meal in their own house that they had missed since they had inherited the title.

I planned to pack my bags and to leave before lunch. Before doing so I was determined to try to find Michael.

When breakfast was over, I went into the kitchen in search of Leyland, who as the collector-in-chief of tips was usually very much on parade at the time that house guests were due to depart. On this occasion, he was not around. Mrs Briely, the cook, told me with some concern that he hadn't been seen since the previous afternoon.

'He usually tells me when he's poorly too,' she said.

'Has anyone tried his room?' I asked.

'I can't be sure about that,' Mrs Briely said, 'but I don't think anyone's been up. I haven't. I've been too busy.'

'Well, I expect that's where he'll be,' I said, with more confidence than I felt.

'What about Mr Michael? Have you seen him?'

'Don't you mean his Lordship?' Mrs Briely asked, tartly.

'Yes, you're right, Mrs Briely, I suppose I do.'

'He's in his room with Mrs.'

'Don't you mean her Ladyship?' I laughed for the first time for several days.

'Oh my gawd, what a thought.' She rolled her eyes upwards. 'Wish you were still here, your Ladyship. We used to have some fun in them days.'

'It's very kind of you, Mrs Briely. I think your memory's playing a few tricks on you, though. I loved it here, of course. You were always so kind to me, though I must admit I never really thought of Greysham as my home. I was more like a guest here.'

'I still wish you and his Lordship hadn't split,' she persisted, 'and now he's gone.' She began to cry loudly. 'There I go again. What shall we do without him? Mr Michael won't be the same thing at all. I hope they find the one what done it soon. It's all so spooky, your Ladyship. I never used to, but I swear these last two nights I've been hearing things. Makes you wonder whether them ghost stories are true. I don't know how long I will be able to stick it out, I'm sure,' she sobbed.

'You must be brave, Mrs Briely,' I said, and then added rather weakly, 'for the memory of his Lordship, if nothing else. I'm going to try to find Mr Michael.'

She smiled through her tears. 'His Lordship, you mean.'

I left her and climbed the staircase. As I approached Michael's room I could hear low voices coming from the other side of the door.

I stood for a moment outside and then knocked hard.

'Who is it?' It was Leyland's voice.

'It's Lady Hildreth. I've come to say goodbye.'

There was a pause. I thought I heard the sound of scuffling in the room. Then the door half-opened slowly. Leyland put his head round. He was unshaven, his hair a mass of tangled, white strands. His eyes were sunken. He clearly had not had much sleep.

'What's going on, Leyland?' I asked.

'It's her Ladyship. She's had one of her turns. She'll be all right.'

The word 'turn' is not one I use. It has no specific medical meaning. It is used by some people to describe a fit, as in an epileptic fit; but so far as I knew, Lucy was not epileptic. Sometimes people seem to mean by 'a turn' the recurrence of a regular but spasmodic illness. If this was the case with Lucy, judging by Leyland's appearance, it must be something quite serious.

'Is there anything I can do to help?' I asked.

He shook his head wearily. 'No, your Ladyship, nothing. No one can help her when she's like this.'

'Like what?'

'Please, your Ladyship, leave us now.'

'Us? Is his Lordship in there?'

Leyland nodded.

'Can I see him?'

'He's sleeping. I'll wake him in half an hour. He won't want to see the others, not now. I suppose he may want to see you, though. In that case, I suggest you meet in the chapel in an hour's time. He can come to it along the underground passage. In that way he won't meet anyone. If he's not there by eleven o'clock, he won't be coming.'

'I suppose that will have to do,' I said. I had forgotten about the underground passage.

I left Leyland for the stables, from where I drove my car round to the front door. I then once again remounted the old staircase and headed for my bedroom. I packed my clothes for the second time that weekend and carried the suitcase out to the BMW. I locked the boot with the suitcase inside it and began to make my way on foot up the drive.

I had always thought the chapel was one of the uglier parts of the Greysham complex. Rebuilt in red brick in Victorian times in a pseudo-Gothic style, it was surrounded by fir trees which added to the darkness of the inside of the building. The chapel had had a rather purposeless existence, certainly since I had known it. It was never used on Sundays, for instance. If any houseguest wanted to go to a service, he made use of the pretty Norman church in the village. It's true John and I had been married in the chapel, but that had itself been rather unsatisfactory, since only about a tenth of the guests had been able to attend the service.

When I arrived at the south side of the building, I noticed with some surprise that the oak door was half open. It had always been kept firmly shut when I lived at Greysham. I went inside and turned on the lights.

Several of the chairs (there were no fixed pews) were

out of alignment. Two were facing in the wrong direction, away from the altar. I remembered my sense of having been taken to the chapel for the strange rendezvous during the night. I wondered for a moment which one of the seats I might have sat on and where my interrogator would have placed himself. For reasons I cannot now fully explain, I began hurriedly to rearrange the chairs, so that within minutes all was back to normal. Ten rows of six chairs were all facing the altar in straight lines again. I looked at my watch. It was a quarter to eleven, fifteen minutes left for Michael to show up.

I was looking at the altar with my back to the door and he must have entered the chapel very quietly. In any case, I didn't notice him until he had put a hand on my waist. I turned and he kissed me on the lips. I felt myself wanting to respond by putting my arms round his back and pulling him towards me. Instead I pulled away from him.

'That was a strange way to arrive,' I said. I needed to give myself time. I knew I was flustered. He had caught me by surprise.

'Still the abominable snow-woman,' he said. 'If you ever melted I think I would go off you.'

'What have you been up to?' I asked, hoping to regain the initiative. 'You were meant to be the host at dinner last night and at breakfast, but you weren't there. Leyland says Lucy's had a turn. What does that mean? I didn't know she was ill.'

He ignored my questions. 'Missed me?' he teased. I felt very uncomfortable. I wanted rather badly to throw myself into his arms, but something held me back, possibly a sense of professionalism. I was on the job and Michael was, after all, a suspect to the murder of his brother.

'Please tell me about Lucy,' I said.

His mood changed quite suddenly. He seemed to

pale. The fun went out of his eyes and he frowned.

'Yes,' he said quietly. 'We don't talk about it very much. In fact, I'd be grateful if you kept it to yourself. It can get quite nasty. It's when she's tense or upset. John's death has been a great shock to her.'

I persisted. 'Is there anything I can do to help?'

He shook his head.

'Leyland and I have got it all under control. What did you want to see me about?'

I had temporarily forgotten that this meeting had been my idea. 'I just wanted to say goodbye and good luck. It's not going to be easy for you.' I didn't feel I sounded totally plausible.

'Thanks,' he said, 'but why do you have to go? We could certainly do with you around at the moment.' I looked away from him and said nothing.

'Will you come back?'

'Will you ask me?' It was a silly, girlish, question. I was leading him on and I should have known better.

'Yes. Probably every weekend until I've seduced you.'

'In that case, the answer's likely to be no.' Now I was teasing him.

'Why, for heaven's sake?'

'Because you're married.'

I thought for one moment he was about to say something like 'she doesn't count'. Instead, he frowned again and he started to make for the door.

'Are you in some sort of trouble, Michael?' I asked.

He paused for a moment. 'Is that what you really wanted to ask me?'

'Yes.'

'Well, the answer, to coin a phrase, is no. Now we're quits. You leave by the door, I'm going by the passage. I'll let you turn out the lights.'

When I emerged from the chapel, it was drizzling. I cursed myself for not having brought my umbrella, or at least a headscarf, and began to half-run down the drive. My dark blue cotton suit was damp by the time I reached my car. I knew that I had no further business to do at that stage with Braithwaite, whose men were still searching the grounds, so I would just leave straightaway.

As I drove slowly away from the house up the drive, I decided not to return immediately to my cottage to prepare for whatever 'the voice' had in store for me. Instead, I would make a small detour – stop for a light lunch at one of my favourite Cotswold pubs, the buttery bar of the Shaven Crown at Shipton-under-Wychwood. I wanted to unwind and think things through for a few moments. I needed especially to think about Michael Hildreth. As usual, I felt that through a process of rationalisation I would be able to work out a total solution to what was admittedly becoming a bit of a problem.

Relationships with men, as far as I was concerned at the time, could always be sorted out in the end by applying your mind to them. By giving yourself plenty of time to mull things over. What one needed to do was to take a deep breath and just plan one's way out; hence the visit to the Shaven Crown. It was just a question of mind over matter; that's all; Michael Hildreth was no different from the rest of them, no different at all.

The buttery was as welcoming as ever. There was a new girl behind the bar who was clearly already a strong attraction for the young bloods from the village. I ordered a gin and tonic and a spinach and bacon lasagne from the bar menu and sat myself down beside the open fire. The scent of slow burning pine logs and the sweet taste of the gin began to relax me.

The fair-haired girl behind the bar had a pretty tan. She tried to ignore a clean-looking middle-class boy in a white shirt and tie who was apparently telling her about his business exploits. 'Hope to go public soon,' I heard him say. She was focusing her attention on a tall curly-haired youth who was also talking to her, telling her about a house he was building. 'Got the bedroom window in,' he said.

'Cheeky,' she replied.

'Where you been then?' he asked her.

'When?'

'These last two weeks; we missed you.'

'Majorca, where else? And I got brown in places you'll never see.'

Not much rationalising going on there, I thought to myself with an inward smile.

Something deeper than a physical – or for that matter, emotional – attraction was drawing me towards Michael Hildreth. Beneath all his bravado was a hunted look about him which I found magnetic. The sense that he was in some sort of trouble had grown on me. What made it the more interesting was that I suspected I was probably the only person in the world to have noticed it. That morning he had displayed many of the classic symptoms of someone under stress: quickly changing moods, unresting eyes, sudden unexpected movements with the hands.

I wondered, not for the first time, what had been the true state of his relations with his brother. Suppose he had been tied up in some way with John's death? Where did that leave me?

CHAPTER FIFTEEN

It was still raining when I emerged from the buttery into the sodden car park. I still had three hours in hand, so I decided to bypass Stow-on-the-Wold and take the minor country roads back. I drove through tiny villages with cottages made of yellow stone, with names such as Kingham, Aston Magna and Batsford; not great tourist wool towns such as Moreton-in-Marsh, Stow-on-the-Wold or Bourton-on-the-Water, nor the classic beauty spots of the Slaughters or the Swells, but idyllic peaceful retreats.

My own village of Chipping Campden falls somewhere in between these categories. Unlike Moreton, Broadway, or Stow, it does not lie alongside a major highway; and yet it is by no means isolated from the world outside. Its several hotels and shops constructed many centuries ago in yellow Cotswold stone are very well patronised by tourists; it is also a town in which locals make their purchases and to which the sheep farmers head for a pint of ale or cider when the sun has set.

My cottage faced onto the main street although my bedroom was at the back, overlooking a tiny garden, which in summer was full of roses and hollyhocks. The walls of the cottage were covered in climbing ceanothus and clematis. On the left, if one faced the house from the street, a neighbour's house was attached; to the right, a small path led up a narrow alley to the garden from a sixteenth century oak gate, which opened in two halves. Through this you could just catch a glimpse of my small lawn surrounded by shrubs and rose bushes.

The little path beside my house was extremely pretty but it had caused me a certain amount of headaches in the past from a security point of view. It was not so much my possessions which had been threatened – although I did own some beautiful antique furniture and some pricey nineteenth century water colours (I'm told I have one of the finest collections of Birket Forsters in the country). It was more my life which from time to time had been at risk.

Despite some unsavoury memories, it always gave me great joy to return home; and of all my properties this was the one I really thought of as home. It was here that I came closest to blending into the landscape. The butcher and the garage-hand and the man who ran the pub down the road all knew me as Jane and I called them Mike and Olly and Fred.

And so it was in a much jollier frame of mind than the one in which I had left Greysham that I parked the car in the narrow road outside the cottage. Across the street someone was working under a mauve 1950s Rolls Royce. I smiled and shouted across, 'How are things?'

The figure rolled out from beneath the car onto the pavement and stood up facing me in oily green dungarees. 'Fine. What about you?'

The Honourable Patricia Huntington was aged somewhat over seventy; she still had lovely flashing black eyes, gorgeous flowing white hair and she was one of the finest mechanics in the county. In addition to the Rolls, she owned a 1930 Buick and a Lagonda, each of which she serviced herself, usually in the street opposite my house. Rumour had it that the only time she had ever lost her good humour was when Olly at the garage had been called in to assist her to move some particularly heavy piece of machinery from one of her cars; the wretched man had slipped and fallen, almost crushing one of his legs, but much more important, virtually destroying the precious piece of equipment. The Honourable Patricia Huntington's expletives as poor Olly hobbled up the road in shame and humiliation are remembered verbatim by the villagers to this day.

Patricia's importance to me had nothing to do with cars. As one of the longest serving agents in the country, she was paid to guard my house. I couldn't blame her for occasionally finding this rather a boring task. Speaking six languages just about word perfect, including Russian and Arabic and having been in her time one of the best marksmen or women in the country, especially with an automatic rifle, she still felt she was destined for greater things than minding my home. For my part, of course, I couldn't have wished for anyone better.

'I'm expecting visitors at around six,' I said. 'I've no idea what they will turn up in or for that matter what they will look like. I should be all right, but keep your eyes out all the same if you will, Pat.'

Patricia Huntington's face lit up. 'Yes ma'am,' she gave a mock American-style salute. 'Thank goodness for a bit of action. I can't tell you how tedious it's been around here for the last few weeks, Jane. Can't you get them to let you come back here more often? It's so much more fun when you're about.' She paused to wipe a blob of oil from her cheek with a filthy yellow rag.

'Even better idea. What about that promise you made to take me with you on a case again?'

I laughed, my mind going back to the last time I had taken Pat with me. On that occasion she had somehow managed to challenge two Arab shepherds to a duel with pistols. As I recollect it, they had fled in bewilderment.

'You're much too valuable here, Pat,' I said 'I'd better go and get ready for my guests.'

As I walked up the little path beside my house, the parish church clock chimed five times. This seemed to stir up a blackbird in the garden at the back; his rather rude whistle was familiar and welcoming.

I entered the house by the back door. As I turned the key I set off a high pitched warning screech, which I knew gave me two minutes in which to turn off the main alarm mechanism.

Once safely inside I turned to my left, switched off the alarm and climbed the narrow winding wooden staircase to my bedroom. I passed my large double bed with its salmon pink and green cover and its old brass bedstead and went straight into the adjoining bathroom. Standing in front of the basin, I gave a sharp twist to the gold plug handle. The mirror above the basin slid right and I extracted my scrambler phone from the cavity behind. A two-minute call to the Office gave me all the permissions I needed and I put the phone back in its place.

I looked at my watch; I just had time to make myself a cup of tea. I went downstairs and put on the kettle. Standing on one of the old three-legged milk stools, I looked round the oak panelled kitchen, with its fifteenth century inglenook fireplace; everything was as I had left it. As I sipped the Lapsang tea I decided on this occasion not to offer Pat a cup; it was rather important for the moment that she continue to watch the front of the house. At five forty-five, my ex-directory phone rang. I took the call from my small dining room at the back of the house.

'Which room are you in?' I thought I recognised the French accent from the night before.

'The dining room.'

'Is that the ground floor room at the back?'

'Yes.'

'Do you have the necessary clearance?'

'Yes.'

'Good. Don't move from where you are until you hear a knock on the double doors separating the room you are in from the one at the front. We will be unmasked as we let ourselves in through the front door, so we will create no suspicion on the part of your neighbours, especially as we have keys. It is important that you do not attempt to view us as we enter the house. If you do, all bets, as they say in your language, will be off.'

The line went dead. Ten minutes later I heard the lock turn in my front door; this was immediately followed by the promised knock on the double doors dividing my drawing room at the front of the house from the dining room at the back. When I swung open the double doors I was confronted by what I took to be the two figures I had met the previous night still disguised in balaclava helmets. By daylight they each seemed smaller than I had remembered them. One was wearing a duffle coat and the other a sheepskin jacket over corduroy trousers.

The American said, 'Place your hands above your head, please, and face towards the wall.' They frisked me thoroughly, and I was glad I had decided not to carry a weapon.

The Frenchman said, 'Sit down, please. Shortly we will reveal our identities. We have orders first to confirm that you will accompany us of your own free will and secondly that you will have no protection. By this we mean you will carry no arms and have no escort.'

'Yes to all of that.'

I thought of Pat Huntington. She would have been

deeply disappointed by that reply.

As if reading my thoughts, the American asked, 'Who were you talking to in the road outside?'

These people were thorough. I decided there was not much point in being defensive with them any longer. I had at last formed a view about the high American voice and the unnaturally low French one. This was a good moment to put my theory to the test; at least it would give me the temporary initiative.

'Why don't you two ladies take off your masks?' I said. 'It would help us to do serious business.'

Neither reacted for a moment. Each seemed suddenly uncertain as to what to do next. Then the American asked quietly, 'Do you agree to come with us immediately, in our car and without leaving our company?'

'Yes, once more.' I wondered briefly what conditions I would not have agreed to. The whole affair interested me more and more. I only hoped it would have some bearing on the disappearance of John Hildreth's body.

'OK, we can take off our covers.'

Each began to roll up from the neck the blue woollen helmet with its eye slits. The American revealed herself to be Sylvia Richards and the French person to be Annabel Silvester.

'Well, well, what a surprise,' I said staring straight at Annabel. 'So you were the two who came to get me last night? I am impressed. Where did you learn to climb a rope so prettily?'

'No more questions. Just come with us,' Annabel said in the deep upper class English accent with which I usually associated her.

'We can discuss nothing further until we deliver you to where we have been told to take you; it should take us not much more than half an hour.'

'Where's your car?' I asked.

'In the car park opposite the King's Head,' Sylvia had dropped her squeaky American accent. I decided I preferred her natural English voice. It reminded me of a case which had taken me for two months around the pubs and clubs of Soho. There had been a particular call-girl whose *nom-de-profession* had been Linda. Her real name had been Janet and Sylvia was the spitting image of her. Each had an earthy loveliness and a quick tongue which people brought up in the back streets of big cities around the world often seem to have in common. Strangely enough, though, when they had been disguised it had been Annabel's deep voice which had sounded the least natural of the two and which had led me to guess their real sex.

Sylvia looked nervously out of the front window at the mauve Rolls Royce shining in the late afternoon sunlight.

'Let's move our arses,' she said. 'We certainly don't want to hang around here any longer than we have to.'

CHAPTER SIXTEEN

As Annabel had predicted, the journey took about half an hour in a very modern-looking Range Rover, with Sylvia at the wheel. They had probably decided that she should drive in order to leave her companion free to deal with me if I became awkward. Annabel certainly looked the stronger of the two, though I knew how deceptive appearances could be. I doubt very much whether many people looking at my rather fragile frame would immediately guess that I can knock most men to the ground, whatever their shape or size. I wondered briefly whether either Annabel or Sylvia would have had training comparable to mine. They certainly each had a very adequate working knowledge of how to climb walls in the middle of the night, to knock down a potential aggressor and to reach for weapons.

Sylvia drove across country, westwards over the northern slopes of the Cotswolds, along narrow lanes lined by low walls made of large blocks of Cotswold stone and through copses of beech and fir where the walls were covered in blackberry and hawthorn bushes. Mainly we passed rolling fields, many of which a few months earlier had been planted with corn but which were now covered in stubble. The fields that were grassed were dotted with thick woolly sheep whose shadows gave a patchwork effect to the luscious landscape.

We drove high above the lovely yellow-stoned village of Broadway, across Snowshill, with the fruit plantations of the Vale of Evesham below us and far to our right, and down towards Toddington. From time to time through the rear window I caught flashes of light behind us. I knew from experience that these depicted the spots where Patricia Huntington was negotiating the road in hot pursuit, probably in the Lagonda. I hoped she was concentrating more on her driving than on keeping up with us. She was a much better mechanic than she was a driver and for the moment I was worried more about her safety than about mine.

Suddenly we turned left off the road and began to climb a steep drive, past a lake to our right.

'I expect you know this house,' Sylvia said.

I shook my head.

'You do surprise me. You'll certainly recognise its owner when you see him.'

Sylvia swung the heavy vehicle with evidently practised ease through the stone archway and into a courtyard. Over a gate on the left I caught sight of a beautiful green lawn.

The house itself was a classic large Cotswold country mansion; its doric pillars in front of the main door suggested that at least the front part was eighteenth century. This would make its origins rather later than most large Cotswold homes. But I must not let my love of English country architecture run away with me.

An old man in a short white coat waited to greet us on the steps leading up to the front door.

'Welcome to Cuts Manor, your Ladyship,' he said. 'The Master and his friends are waiting for you in the drawing room.'

I raised an eyebrow at him but he seemed not to notice. He led the way into the house. We crossed a spacious hall and then entered a long and surprisingly narrow room. Richard Luke, Giles Lester, Bobby Longfellow and two other men were talking around a large open fire. Bobby appeared to be the first to notice me.

'Ah, hello, Jane,' he said. 'Come in. I'm afraid I can't remember whether I have already said good morning to you or not. It doesn't really matter, does it? I hope the girls looked after you all right.'

'You didn't and they did. Is this your house, Bobby? I thought you lived near Birmingham.'

'I do, I do. Stop being boring, Jane, and have a glass of champagne.'

'This isn't Birmingham, unless I've lost all my bump of locality. Whose house is it?' I asked.

'Mine,' said Richard Luke.

'I thought you had blown all your cash on the roulette tables.'

'Not quite, Jane,' Richard spoke in his usual soullessly quiet voice.

Giles Lester giggled loudly.

'What's so funny, Giles?' I asked.

'Nothing, Jane love, nothing. It's just that as Richard is one of the richest men in the world, I thought it ironic that you had him down as a pauper, that's all. No big thing.' He waved a hand at me.

'Well, you lot certainly have come to life. Which one's the voice from last night?' I asked.

'All that later,' Bobby interrupted. 'First things first. I wonder if I could have your permission to dismiss the funny old lady in the Lagonda. The girls have gone down the drive to meet her at the gate and she's terrified the wits out of them. Apparently she's armed to the teeth and has a bloodhound on the back seat.'

'Timmy,' I said. 'Gets very upset.'

'Who, the lady?'

'No, the dog. Probably safer to leave them where they are.'

'As you will,' Bobby said.

'As long as they don't come onto my property,' Luke threatened.

'Let's get on with the business.' Bobby seemed more agitated than usual.

'May I first of all present to you Major François Guillaume of the French Air Force.' He waved expansively at a wiry little man in his late forties who was standing on the other side of the fireplace. The Frenchman came across to me. His eyes were a fanatical blue. He picked up my right hand and kissed it. '*Enchanté*,' he murmured.

'And Colonel Sam Marshall of the United States Air Force,' Richard said. The colonel was a big man with a crushing handshake, which he used generously on me.

'Sam Marshall, USAF. Glad to know you, ma'am.'

Like most Americans, his articulation of the English language was much clearer than ours. His voice was deep and sounded honest.

'You still haven't had a drink, Jane.' As Bobby spoke, I noticed that his bald head was sweating, no doubt because he had been standing too close to the fire.

'Later, please,' I said.

'Later we could all be dead,' Giles Lester said, giggling. 'Only a joke,' he added. I began to wonder whether it had been.

'Look, everyone, I'm expected back in London tonight. It's very nearly seven. Could we get on with whatever you have in mind?'

'Expected by whom?' Bobby's eyes narrowed.

'Not by anyone you would know, Bobby.'

'Won't you stay for dinner? Richard's cook isn't particularly good, but he isn't particularly bad either.'

Richard looked rather pained at Bobby's remark, as

indeed I would have done if it had been my house, but he said nothing.

'I doubt whether I shall have time; but thanks all the same.'

'Well, then,' Bobby conceded, 'there's nothing for it but to get down to business. Shall we sit down?'

He placed himself on the only upright chair. The rest of us sank into an assortment of sofas and heavily cushioned easy chairs. I couldn't help noticing once again how Bobby chose to sit without his feet properly touching the ground.

'With your intelligence, Jane, I'm sure you will have worked out by now that I was the one who talked to you last night.'

'The idea had crossed my mind, Bobby.'

'Let me come straight to the point, if I may, since you say you're in a bit of a hurry. We really would like to know where John is.'

'Join the club,' I said.

'You really expect us to believe that you don't know?'

'You can believe whatever you want; it doesn't concern me too much. In fact, if we go on much longer like this I shall get up and go. This conversation is of no value to me whatsoever.'

'Pity,' Bobby said, 'it would have made life so much simpler.'

'You *do* want to get back to London, don't you?' Giles Lester had introduced a sinister note into the proceedings. I began to wonder whether I would make my appointment that night, or any other appointment for that matter.

'Why don't you just give me your proposition?' I suggested. 'Then we can all get on with whatever we want to do.'

The room fell silent. The Frenchman cleared his throat; for a moment I thought he was about to speak, but it was Bobby who once more got in first.

'All right, dear girl, we'll play it your way for a little while. We will put our proposition, as you call it, to you, but it's going to take quite a bit of your time, I'm afraid. Your boyfriend's going to have to wait rather longer than he's used to. I hope it doesn't upset him. I don't think he likes to be kept waiting.'

Giles Lester smirked.

'Boyfriend?'

'Young Michael Hildreth.' Bobby stared straight at me. 'Quite a catch if it wasn't for the fact that he's married.'

'I'll say this for him. John was right about one thing,' Bobby went on after a pause. 'We've all been working as a team; all of us, that is, who have been staying at Greysham this weekend.'

'Including Michael?' the moment I asked it, I knew the question was a stupid mistake. Bobby, of course, would have picked up the note of urgency in my voice, but to my relief, he let it pass.

'Don't worry,' he said. 'I'll come to him later. May I continue? I believe that John also knew that we've done our little bit of smuggling from time to time. What we don't know – and no doubt you will tell us, Jane – is just how much he knew about exactly what it was that we were carrying around.'

'As a matter of fact, we think you do know exactly what we've been up to,' interrupted Giles Lester. 'We think you know a darned sight more than you are letting on. It's why we decided to meet you like this. I have to tell you I was all for keeping our cover until we had a good idea what sort of a deal we could get out of you. Then it became clear last night that you were either fully in the picture already, or your people soon would be.' Giles was sprawled across a sofa and seemed to have developed a rather unattractive drawl.

Bobby raised his arms, not apparently, in a gesture

of surrender, but to re-establish his leadership.

'Let's begin with Antonio,' he said.

'Antonio was central to our work,' said Richard, from a corner of the room. 'His death practically blew our whole operation. That's why we believe it was one of your people who got him, Jane. One or two of us believe that you personally ordered Antonio to be killed. We are not so sure about John. We're not, as you know, even convinced that he's dead.'

I avoided their eyes and stared straight towards the fire. This was becoming very difficult for me.

Bobby was now sitting upright in his chair. His feet were crossed at the ankles as usual. He was wearing thick woollen socks. He held a glass of champagne and his eyes were fixed on a spot behind my right shoulder.

'The truth is, Jane,' he said, 'that a number of us, in this country, on the continent of Europe, and even in the United States itself, have felt for a long time that the world has become unbalanced.'

'Unbalanced?'

'Yes dear girl, unbalanced; it's not such a bad word. Too much power in too few hands. Which is all right so long as you're a Russian or an American – but even they are getting a bit overawed by it all.'

'Is all this relevant?' I asked.

'Very much so,' Richard answered, so quietly that he was almost inaudible.

Bobby continued. 'Many Americans feel out on their own. On the one hand they find themselves shouldering the burden for all the world's sins – sins for which, by the way, they often don't feel themselves responsible. On the other hand, they are the subject of the world's envy, and even concern, for the power they hold. I'm certainly not prepared to put my life into the hands of the Americans, nor do I see why they should carry the entire burden for me.'

The American air force colonel was nodding. I vaguely recollected that Bobby had recently made a speech along the same lines in the House of Commons.

'Where does all this lead us?' I asked. I was becoming increasingly irritated by having to provide the audience for a regurgitation of one of Bobby's more obscure speeches. He ignored my impatience.

'Europe is an old continent,' he said. 'What is more, in the Common Market it has by far the richest trading block on earth. But the Common Market does nothing for the defence of our sovereignty and for the liberties and the way of life we have built up over thousands of years.'

I had never seen him in full flood before. His eyes had widened and his face, usually pallid, was becoming flushed. 'What we have always needed is for British and French technology to be combined with German finance to create a totally independent European nuclear and space-based defence system.' He stood up and began to pace up and down in front of the fireplace like some latter-day Napoleon.

'And what would the Americans think of this?' I asked. I needed to show some interest, if only to be able to make a progress report to the Office.

'I'm coming to that,' he answered. I noticed that the soles of the sandals he was wearing had deep holes in them. His stomach fell over his grey flannel trousers, which seemed to be held up by a piece of rope.

'The Americans, if they thought about it – and, by the way, they don't think much about Europe these days except as being a drain on their resources – if they thought about it, would love it. It would be the basis for a new alliance of equals and it would cost them a darned sight less money.'

'Where does John come into all this?' I asked.

'John was scraping at the surface of our operations.

To begin with I think he believed we were running drugs or something equally trivial. Quite possibly he killed Antonio in the process of his investigations.'

'I thought you said I had Antonio killed.'

'I hope you aren't playing around with us, Jane. We think you know every little detail of what John was up to. You can trip up and fall flat on your arse by being too clever, you know.' I could see the irritation on Bobby's face at the crudity of this intervention by Giles Lester.

'The point is you were quite right last night, and we have come to see it even more clearly in the last few hours.' Bobby seemed determined now to control the discussion. 'It was only a matter of time before John, no doubt with the assistance of other agents such as yourself, would have uncovered the whole operation. As has already been said, it wouldn't surprise us if every word of what I am telling you is already known to you. If it isn't, it soon would be. We believe John was already onto most of the leads.'

He was watching me closely to try to assess my reaction. I hoped my face was totally impassive.

'It was microfilm that the girls were wandering around the world with.'

'The girls,' as he called them, I had already noticed were absent from all these discussions. I wondered if they were still being terrified by Pat Huntington.

'To skip repeating what you doubtless already know, we were picking up technology from wherever we could find it around the globe. America was bound to be our best source, even if from time to time we had to deal in classified stuff. With Richard's financial help, Giles's business skills, and François's and Sam's contacts, we have gradually put together the technical basis for an all-European ballistic missile defence system.'

Clearly I now had to act out the part he had handed

to me, if only to see how much more there was to come.

'We've never found all this very credible,' I said.

He looked at me in silence and then asked, 'Why not?'

'It has never struck us that you had adequate access to the military or the scientific weight.'

'Ah, that's because you have reckoned without our Air Vice Marshall and his team.'

'Is the Air Vice Marshall serving?' I regretted the question as soon as I had asked it. It had been too direct, revealed a lack of knowledge and deserved the answer it got.

'That, my dear Jane, is the bit I cannot talk about. What you see before you is the team which makes it all possible except for the scientific stuff. We are the practical men. Without us it's all theory.'

'What do you want from me?' I asked.

'First of all, to call off your boss and his American and French counterparts. They're beginning to upset some of my colleagues, especially the military ones. In return, we will stop all our practical operations. I make only two conditions: the first is that you do not try to hunt down our theoreticians, some of whom are very high in government service. The second condition is more of a request – that we are able to debrief before an appropriate team of officials put together by the Joint Defence Staff. This particular scheme may have run into the ground, but I'm determined that the idea will live on. We always intended, of course, to make our findings public. We have wanted to make a point, not of course to make any take-over bid ourselves. That, as you no doubt would point out, being such a level-headed girl, would have been most impractical not to say anti-democratic. One day there will be governments in Europe which will, of their own free will, see that what we are suggesting is the only course which gives our part of the world the proper measure of protection. Our problem the whole time has been to prove it.'

It didn't seem to me that he was in much of a position to make conditions, but I let this pass.

'And what about John Hildreth?' I asked.

'My dear Jane, you know more about John Hildreth than I suspect we ever will.'

'Too true,' Giles said in a loud voice. I realised suddenly that he had been drinking heavily. 'As Bobby says, if we can keep the idea alive, I'm sure there will be money in it one day.' He was looking at Richard.

Bobby turned away from him in apparent distaste and said to me, 'I'll ask the girls to go over to your cottage to collect your car. Oh, and by the way, we are in touch with Michael. Perhaps it would be best if he told you himself how he thinks he fits in.'

CHAPTER SEVENTEEN

I have a habit of tucking the loose strands of my hair behind my left ear when I am deep in thought. I realised I was doing this as I drove east on the A40. Sylvia and Annabel had taken me back to the cottage and I lost no time in starting out for London. What on earth, if anything, was I to make of the meeting with Bobby and his little gang? Was it all complete baloney? There was certainly an element of unreality, of amateurishness about the whole affair and yet, in my business, outlandish explanations are often the correct ones.

It did, of course, occur to me that Bobby was setting up some grotesque distraction. What he had told me had certainly made no contribution at all towards solving the Hildreth murder. Bobby had, in the process of his revelations, by implication exonerated himself and his chums. But that perhaps was precisely what he had intended to do.

How much of all this should I tell the Chief, I wondered. He would be irritated if I presented him with a lot of eyewash. He liked his people to do their own homework before giving him their well-considered analysis. This he would often argue against or even turn down flat, but he liked something sensible to get his teeth into.

I admired the Chief. In fact, if I am truthful, I found

him very attractive. In many ways, he was just my kind of man: a former SAS major, tall, lean, a classicist from Winchester, always courteous, especially to women, but tough as they come, mentally as much as physically. His kiss of death was the returned report, the gentle smile and the words, 'I think this one needs a little more doing to it, Jane' – or Bill, or whoever the unfortunate agent was whose work had not come fully up to expectations.

It was on one of these occasions that I had seriously considered leaving the service. I had asked myself again why I had ever entered it in the first place. I knew the answer then as I know it now.

I smiled to myself as I pulled into a filling station outside Oxford.

When I was a little girl living in Surrey, where my father was a rather successful local solicitor, life had been kind and gentle, not to say genteel. My only fears had been of physical dangers: snakes, falling from heights, hurting myself in a motor accident, death. The fewer there were of events such as these (and I can't honestly remember one physically frightening thing ever having happened to me when I was young), the more fearful of them I became. As I grew up, my terror of physical danger became, if anything, worse.

And then, quite suddenly, soon after my marriage broke up, I became obsessed with the idea of overcoming and conquering this phobia. It developed into the all-consuming challenge of my life. I'm not exaggerating when I say it became for me almost the reason for my existence. It was what I was here to do, to overcome the fear of physical danger. One thought I had was to remarry for the sole purpose of going through the pain of having children. Somehow I had never found quite the man I wanted to make this experience possible. So I joined the cosmetics company and travelled widely in search of physical adventure. It had never come my way in that occupation.

It was only by chance that I met a man who knew my father and who indirectly introduced me to the security services for which I work now. I started as a police officer. All my basic training was in police work, but for the past four years I have been seconded by the Metropolitan Police to the Foreign and Commonwealth Office, against whose head count I now appear. All very confusing until one appreciates that much of the criticisms of our security services in the past arose out of the rivalry and lack of cooperation between MI5 and MI6. The Office I work for tries to put this right these days.

People sometimes say it is only men who go out to prove their physical courage: not true as far as I'm concerned, and I think there are a lot of women around like me. It's not that I don't get frightened any more. I have been on jobs when I am so scared that I could scream, and sometimes do. What I do get is a tremendous satisfaction when the task is over and I have proved, once again, that I can overcome my fear. As I get older, I am constantly surprising myself about just how far I can push myself physically.

Some of this must have been going through my mind as I headed along a dual carriageway towards the M40. I suddenly tensed as I became aware that a red sports car had drawn level with me in the outside lane and was moving in parallel with my BMW. For a moment I wished that I was still being tailed by the redoubtable Pat Huntington (she had followed us as we left Richard's grounds, and I had told her when we reached the cottage that she needn't follow me to the city). However, I relaxed at once when I saw that the dark-haired young driver was smiling at me and pointing to the verge of the road in an attempt to make me pull up. I smiled back and shook my head. He raised both hands in the air, accelerated into the distance and after a few minutes was out of sight.

I felt a little deflated. He had looked rather fun. There were times when I wished I had it in me to unbend just a little bit more, and as Antonio would have put it, 'go mad'. 'One day,' I muttered to myself, 'one day.'

My mind returned to the question of what I should tell the Chief. I decided on this occasion he would have to have the lot. It might irritate him not to be given a more conclusive report; but there were so many loose ends. There were also my personal relationships with the people involved. Any analysis would not only, therefore, be incomplete, it was also likely to have a subjective bias to it. Better this time to give him a straight chronology of what I had learnt.

I decided in particular I couldn't hold back on anything of what Bobby had said, if only because it implicated the Office – about which he seemed to have an uncomfortably wide knowledge. Bobby's foreign policy ramblings were certainly proper material for the Chief.

My mind wandered back to Bobby's remarks about John. If it proved to be correct that John had been one of our active agents, it put my marriage to him in rather a peculiar light. I wondered briefly whether our wedding might have been part of a bizarre scheme dreamt up by the Chief's predecessor. My thoughts became more and more fanciful as I reached the centre of London. I turned off the M40 at the Paddington Junction and a few minutes later entered Hyde Park at Lancaster Gate. I looked at my watch: it was almost midnight. To my left, the moon was reflected on the black surface of the Serpentine. On the south side of the park I turned left towards Knightsbridge and then right into Montpelier Square. I was relieved to find a resident's parking space just outside my house.

I lifted a bag from the boot of my car and approached

my front door. As I did so, I realised that a branch of the old wisteria tree which climbed the main wall of the house had half broken off and was blocking my way. With some difficulty I wrestled with the wizened obstacle. At last it snapped in my fingers and I was able to turn the key.

Just at that moment, the phone in the entrance hall began to ring. I closed the door behind me and, without turning on the lights, lifted the receiver.

A voice said, 'Jane?'

'Yes.'

'Will you have dinner with me tomorrow?'

It was Michael.

CHAPTER EIGHTEEN

The Chief was clearly distracted by other work when I finally managed to have an interview with him at three o'clock the following afternoon. He seemed singularly uninterested in what I had to tell him about Bobby Longfellow.

'Rich men playing games bore me,' he said. 'Why the charade during the night? Perhaps he genuinely does believe you killed Hildreth and he wanted to frighten you into admitting it. Perhaps, like most men, he finds you extraordinarily attractive and it was his way of getting his kicks. I'm told he's a bit like that.'

'I think I may have persuaded him to start talking openly to us,' I said, hopefully.

'Possibly,' he replied.

'What about John?' I asked. '*Did* he work for us?'

The Chief's answer was infuriatingly non-committal.

'Stay working on a need-to-know basis, Jane, and you'll keep being a great asset to us here.'

I knew I would get no further, at least not today. No point in pursuing it. 'Thank you for everything, sir,' I said.

The Chief frowned. 'You do still like it here, I hope? No question of your wanting to go back to full-time policing?'

'Of course I like it.'

'Thank God for that. There hasn't been much good news around here lately. I do hope the body turns up soon.'

Was this his way of expressing sorrow for the death of my former husband? If so it was a funny kind of sympathy. I wondered for a moment whether the Chief had ever in his entire life gone wild with emotion, whether he was even capable of doing so; had he ever panicked or burst into tears or shouted in rage? I didn't give the matter an excessive amount of thought as I had little doubt what the answer was. The Chief might look a nice man. In actual fact he was as cold and as ruthless – and I have to admit as exciting – a man as you could find.

'Thank you,' I said again and rose to leave.

'Oh, Jane,' he called out, as I reached the door. 'I don't want to interfere in any way; just as one chum to another. Please don't take it amiss, will you? But I've always found Michael Hildreth rather an unsavoury character. I know its largely a question of personal taste, but I just thought you ought to know, that's all.'

I knew I was blushing as I turned the door handle – I hoped it was more out of anger than embarrassment, though it was probably a bit of both. The Chief evidently numbered mind-reading amongst his many other accomplishments, or perhaps I, too, was under surveillance.

In any event, I met Michael that night at the place he had suggested: La Popotte in Walton Street. 'A bit off-beat,' he had said. 'Nobody we know ever goes there, and I believe there may even be some plan to pull it down; but until they do, the food's good enough.'

Michael was sitting in a corner seat by a window when I arrived at the restaurant just after eight. He was frowning as he looked across the road at what I knew to be a special services police station; I had been attached there for a short period three or four years earlier.

I was wearing a short evening dress with a rather low front. I saw Michael before he spied me, and he seemed tense, but when he saw me enter the room, his face seemed to relax a little. He rose and pulled out the table so that I could sit on a soft seat on the inside, and placed himself opposite me. A single lighted candle was balanced rather precariously in a silver holder between us.

'I'm glad you're on time,' he said. 'I never like women who purposely mess you around by being late. It's so unnecessary and starts the evening off on a bad note.' Something came back to me that Bobby Longfellow had said the evening before about Michael's taste for punctuality.

'You're lucky,' I said. 'I'm known for being late, though I try very hard not to be.'

'I'm very honoured. What will you drink?' Michael seemed to be going out of his way to be nice; I was enjoying myself already.

'Campari and soda, please.'

'You like a bitter taste.' And then for a while neither of us spoke. There was no awkwardness about our silence. Michael stared at the table. He was wearing a double breasted suit and deep blue tie against a striped blue shirt. He seemed to be avoiding my eyes, which in a strange way pleased me; I wasn't quite ready to become too intimate with him. I felt very comfortable, though in the end it seemed somehow natural for me to make the running.

'What's all this about?' I asked.

'I need to talk to you. Shall we order first?'

As he lowered his head over the menu, the long strands of his fair hair fell across his forehead. I thought about the Chief's warning.

A tall glass of bubbly red liquid was placed in front

of me and Michael was given what I took to be a gin and tonic. It was clearly not his first.

'I hear you were at Luke's place on Sunday,' he said.

'How do you know?'

'Bobby told me.'

'You keep in close touch with him, do you?'

'Not in the way you are thinking, Jane. Of course, he tries every so often to get me to join his outfit; but no way – it's just not my scene. Nutty as fruitcakes, the lot of them.'

I wanted to believe him.

'Do you think one of them killed John?' he suddenly asked.

'I'm not sure.'

He looked at me intently and seemed to be weighing up carefully what to say next. When he eventually spoke, I had a feeling that it was not what he had originally intended to say.

'Strange fellow, Bobby Longfellow. Brilliant of course, but totally wasted. I can't make up my mind whether he will drink or eat himself to death.'

'I thought he had a system for cutting off just in time.'

He ignored that. 'Bobby is capable of having killed John out of spite,' he said.

'Bobby?'

'Yes. It was John, after all, who rumbled his silly plot, if you can call it that. There was never anything very sinister in it, you know. Bobby just wanted to make a point. Giles hoped to get a quick buck out of it some way – I can't think how – and Richard just went along for the ride.'

'And Annabel and Sylvia?'

'Groupies,' he said. 'In it for the kicks.'

'You know an awful lot about it all for someone who opted out,' I said.

For the first time that evening he looked straight at

me. He was frowning, as he had been when I arrived. There was the same troubled look in his eyes that I had noticed at Greysham. He took hold of one of my hands and said nothing. Suddenly, for a brief moment I felt awkward. Michael was desperately attractive. I dropped my eyes away from his.

Then I heard him say, 'None of this is what I wanted to talk about.'

I remember shivering, as I do when I am very nervous. I wondered what on earth was coming.

'Do you know of anyone who could put me onto a good clinic abroad, say in Switzerland? It's not a world I know much about.'

'You don't know Switzerland?' I asked with some disappointment. I suppose deep down I had hoped for something rather more exciting than this.

'No, Switzerland I know well, you chump. I ski there twice a year, after all. Clinics, I mean. I don't know a thing about clinics.'

'What on earth for?' Although I had to ask the question, I was not totally unprepared for his answer. I began almost to have a feel for the way the conversation was reading.

'Lucy,' he said. She needs looking after. She's in a bad way. I can't cope with her any more. It's all too much. Even Leyland has threatened to leave if he has to look after her much longer.'

'What's wrong with the poor girl?' I asked. 'Is it depression?'

'Oh, yes, all of that.'

'Has she seen doctors?'

'Of course.'

'Well, why don't you get her doctor to advise about a clinic?'

'Because she now refuses to see any more doctors. By law nobody can be forced into medical care unless they are thought to be a danger to themselves or to other people.'

'Is she?'

He paused for a moment. His eye began to twitch and I thought he was about to cry. I felt myself squeeze his hand. He flicked his hair with a movement of his head.

'I don't know. I really don't know.'

For much of the rest of the evening we ate in silence. Michael had been right; the food was good. The vegetables, in particular, were fresh and not overcooked. As I remember, he ordered smoked salmon and steak and I had avocado soup and veal.

I felt at ease with him; to be truthful it was more than that: he excited me. I think it was his new vulnerability which made him so appealing. At one moment I confess I even regretted having brought my own car; it meant we could not leave together. Later I knew it had been better that way.

When the time came to go, I said, 'I'll see if I can find someone who knows about clinics for the emotionally ill. Switzerland may not be the best place. It sounds to me as if Lucy needs more than fresh air and a good rest. From what you've said, or perhaps more from what you haven't said, she probably needs very special medical help quickly and before it's too late.'

Michael seemed very relieved; I had grasped the essence of what he had been trying to tell me.

'You've got it in one,' he said gravely and kissed me gently on the forehead. I squeezed his arm and we parted on the pavement outside the restaurant.

When I returned home, I poured myself a whisky and soda, something I had not done for years. After watching the late news headlines on the BBC, I went up to my bedroom and slipped out of my dress. I was just about to turn on the bath taps when my bedroom telephone rang.

'Jane?'

It was a woman's voice – one that I couldn't immediately recognise.

'Yes. Who is it?'

'I am sorry to bother you at this time of night, but it's so urgent. I just had to call you.'

'I'm sorry, but who is speaking?'

'Lucy. Lucy Hildreth.'

'Lucy! What is it? What can I do?'

'I need help, desperately. We all need help.'

'Where are you?'

'At Greysham.'

I thought of her in that great house, where only four nights previously her brother-in-law had been murdered and where his body probably still lay.

'Lucy, what exactly is the problem? Are you frightened? I'm sure we can fix for Leyland or Mrs Briely to keep you company.'

There was a scream on the phone. I had to hold the receiver away from my ear. 'Lucy, Lucy, are you there?'

She was sobbing. I heard her wail, 'Not Leyland, not Leyland. You don't understand. Nobody understands.'

Then suddenly she went silent.

'Lucy?'

Her voice had gone deeper than I had ever heard it. She was almost growling as she said, 'You won't tell Michael? He would kill me if he knew.'

'Knew what?'

Now she was laughing. 'That I had phoned you.'

'Lucy, what do you want me to do?'

'Come and see me tomorrow morning. You will be very interested in what I have to tell you and even more in what I have to show you.'

'Where? At Greysham?'

'Yes.'

'But what happens if Michael finds out?'

'He won't. He won't be back for two days.' There was a cunning in her voice.

'OK,' I said, 'but will you go to sleep now?'

'I might.' Her voice had risen in pitch; she sounded like a little schoolgirl. 'What time will you come?' she pleaded.

'About eleven.'

'I'll be waiting for you.' She faded into a whisper. Then there was a click and the phone went dead.

CHAPTER NINETEEN

When I pressed the bell at Greysham the next morning, it was Leyland who opened the door. He did so slowly, blinking into the daylight. He was unshaven and tieless.

'I have come to see her Ladyship,' I said.

'She's not up yet,' he said sullenly.

It was at that moment that I caught sight of Bobby Longfellow standing in the hall. 'Hello, Jane,' he said. 'Didn't expect to see you here.' His face was pale and without emotion.

I stared at him. After a moment's silence, I said, '*You* here?'

His smile was grim. 'I take my pleasure where I find it.'

'You mean – you and Lucy?'

'If you want to put it like that,' he said.

'Where is she?' I asked.

'In bed. Don't disturb her just now. She's not very well. I shall be gone in a moment. I expect she will be down soon after. In the meantime, why don't we have a cup of coffee together in the South Room?'

'I came to see Lucy,' I said.

Ignoring me, he led the way out of the darkness of the hall into the South Room. He was wearing an olive green open-necked shirt and dirty white baggy trousers. As I followed him I noticed a dark patch of sweat on his back.

'What's really going on, Bobby?'

'My dear Jane, I was just about to ask you the same thing.'

He walked over to the fireplace and pressed a bell, and then sat himself in one of the upright chairs. Deliberately, he took a cigar from his shirt pocket.

'There are a lot of questions each of us would like to put to each other. Shall I begin?'

I had stopped listening to him. I was beginning to become genuinely concerned about Lucy. Perhaps she had been under some real physical danger when she phoned me last night. The mention of Leyland had seemed to terrify her. Not for the first time at Greysham I wished I had come armed.

'For a start, why did you and Michael dine together last night?'

Before I could answer him, Leyland appeared at the door. His eyes had a haunted look. Seeing him again I noticed that his skin had gone grey. Two hollows marred his cheeks.

'Coffee for two, Leyland, there's a good chap.'

As Leyland retreated, Bobby said, 'Where were we? Ah yes, my dear Jane – with Michael. I was wondering what you two were up to; quite natural inquisitiveness, don't you think?'

'We met to talk over some business. Not very interesting, I'm afraid, Bobby. No use for your fertile, not to say perverted, imagination.' I warmed to the theme.

'As we are on the subject, let me tell you I think it was the kinky streak in you which led you to order the two girls to bring me blindfolded to you in the chapel the other night. When we have found who is responsible for John's death, we will deal with you. A small-time pervert with a lot of big talk, that's what you are. I don't think you killed John. I don't think you have the guts. But I wouldn't be surprised to find that in some twisted way you were at the bottom of it.'

'Careful, Jane,' he warned. 'I can get very angry if I am pushed too far. I happen to believe that either you or Michael murdered John. So don't start getting rude with me. Whoever it was, I'm damned sure you know. What, by the way, was the answer from your boss to my little proposition?'

Leyland entered with a coffee pot and cups on a silver tray.

'Thank you, Leyland. Just put it down on the table, would you,' Bobby ordered. As the butler left, he stared spitefully at me.

'You asked me a question,' I said.

'I remember.'

'The answer is that my boss thought you were an inconsequential little twit.'

'That's what he may have told you. It's not what he said to me when we had a little drink together last night.'

I regret to say that I must have flinched at this.

'Surprised?' he asked. 'Bill Singleton and I are old friends. The truth, my dear Jane, is that the establishment is rather pleased with me. I knew they would be. They hate the Americans, you know. I don't share this hatred, but I do feel it's time the alliance was more equal. I've proved my point, now someone else can take over. Do you love Michael?'

I turned away from him towards the window. To my surprise the helicopter was still standing on the far side of the lawn. Bobby seemed to have a knack of anticipating my thoughts. 'It's not working,' he said. 'Michael couldn't use it to come up to see you yesterday. He wanted to, but it wouldn't start up.'

He poured out two cups of coffee and brought one over to me.

'Ever thought what Lucy might make of your affair with Michael?' he asked.

'We're not having an affair.'

'You could have fooled me.'

I wanted to ask about him and Lucy, but felt this would be sinking to his level.

'Are you sure Lucy's in her room?' I asked. The whole situation at Greysham was beginning to make me feel very uncomfortable.

'I think you should know,' he said, 'that Lucy is a very unhappy person.'

'That's quite obvious.'

He looked at me through half-closed eyes, his cigar in one hand and a cup in the other. 'Michael's behaviour hasn't helped.' He spoke with venom. The implication was that my behaviour hadn't helped either.

'I think I will go and find her,' I said.

'I wouldn't do that. I've just told you, she's not well.'

As I rose to leave the room, Bobby also got up and went over to the mantelpiece to press the bell. I left him and went out into the hall. In front of me I could see the long dark passage which led to the main staircase. There was no one in sight as I reached the floor upstairs. I assumed that Lucy would be in the same room that Michael had occupied three nights before. I approached the door with increasing anxiety. When I turned the handle it was locked. I put my ear to the door to listen, but there was no sound. As I turned around, my eyes met the sullen glare of Leyland.

'Can I help you, your Ladyship?' he asked, in a voice which was almost hoarse.

'Why is this door locked, Leyland?'

'For her Ladyship's own protection, your Ladyship.'

'Is Mr Longfellow any part of this, Leyland? I need to know. It's important.'

'Mr Longfellow has just left, your Ladyship.'

'That isn't what I asked, Leyland.'

He remained silent. The whites of his eyes shone dully out of the gloom of the landing.

'Lady Hildreth asked me to come and see her and I mean to do so,' I said. 'Has she locked herself in from the inside?'

'No, I have the key,' the old butler told me.

'Then give it to me.'

He fumbled in the pocket of his frayed pin-stripe trousers and pulled out a small key. I took it from him and turned the lock in the door.

As I entered Lucy's room, she was sitting in a high-backed chair facing out of the window. She was dressed in a white cotton gown and her long brown hair fell uncombed over her shoulders. She didn't move as I approached her and for a moment I thought she was dead. Then without looking at me, she said in a quiet, lifeless voice, 'I'm glad you've come, Jane. Tell Leyland to go away. I won't need him for the time being.'

I looked at Leyland, who stood motionless, glaring at me. I remembered again the effect that his name had had on Lucy the night before.

'You heard what Lady Hildreth said, Leyland.' I tried to sound more confident than I felt. There was a fury in his eyes. I thought for one moment he was going to strike me. Instead, he suddenly turned round and shuffled out of the room.

CHAPTER TWENTY

She lifted her arm and pointed out of the window.

'See that helicopter over there? It doesn't go. It won't fly.'

I thought of telling her that Bobby had already told me it was out of order; instead, I asked, 'How do you know it won't?'

She laughed and began to twirl her hand in an upward spiral, as if imitating a helicopter taking off.

'I tried to fly it,' she said.

'And it wouldn't work?'

'No. I *said* it was broken. But I found something,' she added slyly.

'Found what?'

'I'll show you if you come with me. Can you fly it?'

'I'm afraid not, though I wouldn't mind learning.' This was true and still is. 'Do you want to show me what you've found now?'

She seemed suddenly to change her mind. She began to shake her head. 'No, I want to talk a little more first,' she said. 'People don't talk to me very much these days.'

'Bobby talks to you.'

'Yes, yes, Bobby talks to me.' For the first time, there was genuine animation in her voice.

'I saw Bobby when I arrived,' I said.

She turned to face me; once again I saw how pretty

she was when she was excited. I think I would go further – she was beautiful.

'Was he nice to you?' she asked.

'Not very. I have to admit, I don't think he likes me very much.'

At this, she seemed to switch off. For a moment, she was silent, then she said, 'I want to tell you who murdered John. But first I'll show you what I found. Let's go.' All this was the more astonishing for being said in a rush. She had become like a breathless little schoolgirl.

'Shouldn't you put on a coat if we're going outside?' I couldn't help treating her like an invalid.

'I'm very warm. Here, feel my hand.'

I took her hand in mine: it felt bony and very cold.

'Are you sure you're OK, Lucy?'

'I'm fine,' she said, smiling thinly. Holding my hand, she led me out of the room, down the stairs and into the garden through a door at the back of the house. Looking back as we began to walk across the lawn, I was sure I saw Leyland peering at us from between half-drawn curtains in the dining room. When we began to approach the helicopter she quickened her pace. The maroon machine with its single rotor blade seemed to excite her. She was breathing deeply, apparently unaffected in her thin dressing gown by the cold autumn air.

When we reached the helicopter she paused, seemingly struck by a new uncertainty. I felt her tremble. 'You go first,' she said very quietly.

'What do you want me to do?'

'Get into it,' she said.

'Then what?'

'I'll tell you. Please get up there now.' She was becoming agitated again.

I opened the cockpit door and pulled myself up until I stood at the edge of the opening.

'Can you see anything?' Lucy called from the grounds.

'What am I looking for?' I shouted back.

'Look, look around you, look.'

And then I saw what she wanted me to see: a white silk scarf, arranged in a bow around the joy stick. Sick at heart, I could make out the white monogram from where I balanced myself: J.L.H.

'Find it?' she called.

'Yes, Lucy, I've found it.'

'I tied the bow. It's pretty, don't you think?'

I jumped down from the aircraft and caught hold of her.

'Let's go back to the house,' I said. 'We've obviously got things to talk about.' She did not resist as we walked briskly back the way we had come.

'Let's talk in the South Room,' I said. 'It'll be warmer in there than in your bedroom.'

By the time we reached the South Room, she had begun to cry and I began to wonder how coherent she was going to be. I felt the coffee pot which Bobby had ordered an hour or so earlier. It was still just warm. I poured some tepid black coffee into the cup I had used and handed it to her. She seemed to calm down.

'What do you want to tell me?' I asked.

'Haven't you guessed yet?'

'I've got one or two ideas, but I must hear what you've got to say first.'

'I wish Bobby were here,' she said.

'Lucy, you must get whatever it is that's worrying you off your chest.'

'Jane, could I have some milk?' she asked, like a child. I went over to the silver tray and collected a Worcester china milk jug. She began to cry again as I poured the milk into her cup, which she held close to her with both hands. Then we sat in silence for what must have been several minutes. Suddenly she asked, 'Where should I begin?'

'I'm afraid only you can decide that, Lucy.' I hoped I hadn't sounded too harsh. I desperately wanted to find a way of helping her to tell her story, but couldn't think of one. Only she knew how to start. Suddenly she began to talk very fast, in such a low voice that I found it quite difficult to hear all of what she was saying. The main points, however, were not hard to pick up.

'That was John's scarf in the chopper,' she said. 'Doesn't that tell you who killed him?'

'Michael? For the title and all that goes with it – the estates, the high living?'

'What else?' Lucy said. 'It's so simple, so straightforward. You would have seen it yourself, Jane, if you had not been so besotted by him. You've always lusted after my Michael. If it weren't for Bobby, dear darling Bobby, I would probably have slit your throat by now.'

She half rose out of her seat; for a moment, I thought she was going to attack me. Then she sank back down again, frowning and sighing.

This time it was my turn to keep silent. There seemed no point in arguing with her, poor demented girl.

'Don't you want to know what he did with John's body?' she suddenly asked. 'John was your husband once. One might have thought you would take more interest in what happened to his remains.' She half turned away then looked at me out of the corners of her eyes. Then she answered her own question. 'The wedding in Norwich – remember? Michael took the body with him and threw it out as far into the North Sea as he could manage.'

As she stopped talking the door opened and Bobby Longfellow stood on the threshold. 'What will you do now?' he asked me.

'What *you* should have done all along. Inform the police.'

CHAPTER TWENTY-ONE

As I drove back to London, I have to admit I was not entirely motivated by professional curiosity when I decided that I would try to get to Michael before the police did. Assuming that what Lucy had told me was true; if they were going to take him away, I wanted at least to have one last talk with him on my own. Perhaps she had been right. Perhaps I had always been besotted by Michael.

It was about half past two when I reached central London. I decided to drive straight to Michael's club, Boodles in St James's. There was an off-chance he might still be having a late lunch there, or perhaps playing a quick game or two of backgammon before returning to his office in the City.

I parked my car in St James's Square and walked through side streets, past the Economist building, into the Ladies' entrance of Boodles.

I approached the woman behind the cashier's desk in the dining room and asked her to ring through to the main part of the Club to find out whether Lord Hildreth was still there. She was a little greying lady with large black-rimmed glasses and a kind smile. 'Of course, madam, that'll be the new Lord Hildreth,' she said. 'Lord Michael. Terrible business about his brother. They haven't found the body yet. I don't know how they can tell for sure that he's dead. I read all about it in the *Evening Standard* last night. I would have thought young Mr Hildreth would have had to wait for his brother's body to be found before he started to use the title.' Then, quickly, she added, as if she had overstepped the boundaries of propriety (which she had), 'Of course, it's none of my business, rather rude of me to have mentioned it. It's just that everybody's discussing nothing else in the Club. I'll ring through straight away to see if he's there.'

He was. When he heard who it was waiting for him in the Ladies' section, he said he would come downstairs immediately. He arrived flushed and a little dishevelled. He had obviously been drinking.

'Jane, how nice to see you. Have you got time for a brandy or a coffee or something?'

'No, thank you. Can we just find somewhere quiet where we can talk?'

'What about over here?' he said, pointing to an empty corner in the anteroom. 'I've never seen you look so deadbeat, Jane, love. What's the problem?' We sat down close to each other.

'I think you are about to be arrested,' I said.

'What on earth for?'

'The murder of John Hildreth.' By giving him this warning, I knew I had already broken my professional bond. I half expected Michael to jump to his feet and make his escape. Had he done so there was nothing much I could have done to stop him. Instead, he seemed to sober up.

'What on earth makes them think that?' he asked.

'Lucy.'

'Lucy?'

'She's told us everything, including how you dumped the body out at sea.'

Michael slumped back in his seat. He pushed his long legs out in front of him and loosened his tie.

'I suppose it was bound to catch up with me in the

end,' he said. 'What do I do now? Report to the nearest police station, I suppose. Where is that from here, Jane, do you know?'

'Oh, Michael, I don't know.' I was sobbing. It was the first time I had cried in front of a man for years.

'I imagine Bow Street will do, that can't be very far away. Everybody seems to end up at Bow Street at some point. I spent a night there after some mad party about ten years ago.'

'Oh, Michael, Michael, why, why?'

He didn't seem to be listening to me any more. 'Will you drive me round?' he asked. 'Where's your car?'

'In St James's Square.'

'Good, that's not far away. Let's have a brandy for the road, as they used to say before they brought in the daft drink-drive laws.'

'Let's go now,' I said. 'I don't think I can take much more of this.'

We left the club. I held his hand as we walked for five minutes in drizzling rain to my car. When we reached it, he slumped into the passenger seat beside me. I turned on the ignition, and switched on the windscreen wipers.

'I did it for her,' he said suddenly.

'Did what, darling?' I heard myself ask.

'Threw the body out to sea. I did it to protect little Lucy.'

'I don't understand.'

'Nobody will,' he said.

'I don't understand why you murdered John to protect Lucy.'

'Lucy murdered John. I got rid of the body.' He was shaking. I turned the car ignition off. I needed to talk to him much more before I took him to the police.

CHAPTER TWENTY-TWO

I looked over to him. His face was white and he was staring straight ahead through the windscreen. The rain clouds had darkened the inside of the car. I couldn't make out exactly the look in his eyes, but his strong features, prominent handsome nose and his firmly-set generous mouth were silhouetted against the window on the passenger side.

'Why did Lucy murder John?' I asked him.

He thought for a moment. I wondered whether perhaps he had decided not to answer me, then he said, 'She's mad, schizophrenic; has been for years. No one ever managed to cure her. Tried everything: shock treatment, medication – nothing has ever worked.' His speech was disjointed; he seemed to be finding it hard to breathe.

'But that doesn't make her a killer,' I said.

'I'm afraid it does. You asked yesterday evening whether she was dangerous; well she is, very dangerous; specially since she became obsessive about John.'

'About John? Why?'

She formed the view that he killed Antonio. I haven't the faintest notion where she originally got the idea; possibly Bobby put it into her head.'

'Bobby?'

'I'll come to him in a minute. For all I know Lucy was

right. Perhaps John did murder Antonio, or at least order his death; God only knows what John's motives might have been. Could have been any number of things: jealousy about Elizabeth, something to do with his job – he was certainly some sort of government agent, that I do know. It really doesn't matter very much now, does it?'

I broke in, 'If it had been anything to do with his job, I think I would have heard about it by now. If John really did murder Antonio then it was much more likely to have been because of Elizabeth.'

Michael thought for a moment. When he spoke again, he seemed to be choosing his words with great care. 'I don't like what I'm about to tell you, Jane, because it puts John in such a bad light. It makes him look such a phoney, some kind of monster, for arranging the Greysham weekend; but what you have just said about Elizabeth being the most likely motive for his killing Antonio ties up in another way. Remember the suicide note he left? The one you found on his body? Well, I have to tell you, that was quite genuine – genuine, that is, in the sense that he wrote it himself.'

'What are you saying?' I was deeply shocked. 'How do you know I found that note on him?' This was the one piece of information connected with my discovery of John's body that I had consciously withheld from Michael. I was appalled at the implications of what he had just said.

He appeared to show some sensitivity for this when he turned to me, put a hand on my arm and for the first time looked straight into my eyes. He spoke very quietly and deliberately; there was something suddenly a little sinister about his voice.

'I saw you, my dear.'

I tried to keep as calm as possible. 'I find that hard to believe.'

'I watched you come down the stairs, though I didn't actually see you trip over the body. By that time I had escaped into a room down the passage. As a matter of fact, I was worried you might hear me open and close the door.'

'I did,' I said sombrely. Michael's role was beginning to confuse me. Against all my inner wishes, I was becoming deeply suspicious of him. 'What on earth were you up to?'

'May I come to that in my own time? I want to be sure that I get the chronology of events right. First, the suicide note: John wrote it all right, of that I'm sure, but not at the time of his death. As a matter of fact I found it some weeks earlier in one of his shooting jackets. We often used to borrow each other's sporting clothes when we were both at Greysham. I thought the note was some sort of bad joke at the time, it was so crude and stupid. I had meant to tease John about it, but somehow it went out of my mind. Sounds a bit silly now, doesn't it? Anyway, I must have left it lying around in my bedroom and presumably Lucy found it. That, of course, was at least one good reason why she believed that John murdered Antonio.'

He paused for a moment as if trying to decide something before proceeding.

'Now I suppose we'll never know whether John ever actually intended to do away with himself. If he did, he must have changed his mind. He certainly didn't commit suicide last weekend.'

Michael's voice faded away. There was so much that he had left unclear – especially about his own part in the affair. I had a duty to press him now, even if I had no wish to do so.

'You say Lucy killed John to revenge in some way the death of Antonio. But she hardly knew Antonio. I confirmed that much with her myself when I spoke to her at Greysham on the Saturday morning.'

'I know. That's what I kept telling her, but as I say, she became obsessive about his death. It began to matter desperately to her, a question of warped morality. I tell you she's mad. She evidently began to feel it was her moral duty to put right the injustice which had been done.'

'By killing John? Michael, do you realise that she is willing to testify that it was you who murdered your brother. Does she hate you so much?'

At first I thought he hadn't heard me. He continued in what was now a flat monotone; he seemed to be speaking more to himself than to me. 'There is one other fact you should know about Lucy and this may help to explain her attitude to me. She has become totally infatuated with Bobby Longfellow. In some weird way, he seems to have found a method of getting through to her. I have no idea how. I don't particularly want to know now, though it hurt me terribly when I first found out that there was something between them. I don't even know whether they are lovers or whether Bobby has practised any of his kinky arts on her. My problem is that I love her. I always will.'

I stared at him. I had become accustomed to the gloom and I could now see that his eyes were glistening; tears were rolling down his cheeks. I felt embarrassed, intruding on his privacy.

'Anyway,' he whispered, 'in the last year Bobby has meant everything to her. I think John's attack on Bobby at dinner and his promise to expose him released a triggering device in Lucy's mind.'

I remembered the sudden animation in Lucy's face that night.

'The rest followed on in a kind of lunatic logic.' He put both hands over his face so I could only just make out what he was saying.

'She found some pretext to invite John for a drink

late at night in the drawing room; not satisfied with poisoning him, she tried to attack his throat as he lay dying. I can't imagine where she got the poison – possibly from one of her suppliers.'

'How do you know all this, Michael? How can you possibly be so sure that she killed John?'

'I was there. I saw her. Any more questions?' He was glaring at me in anger.

'None, Michael, except the obvious. How did you get there and what part did you play?'

'She must have disturbed me when she got out of bed. I woke up to find she had gone and went downstairs to look for her. I arrived in the drawing room just in time to pull her away from John's throat but too late to keep him alive. She pushed the suicide note into my hand, hissing, "That's how it happened – unless you're going to take the blame." I told her to go upstairs to bed like a good girl. I would think of a way of sorting everything out. I felt sure that no one would believe it was suicide and all I could come up with was a plan to dump John's body as far out to sea as possible. After sitting looking at him for what I suppose must have been about an hour, I decided to carry him straight out to the helicopter.

'When you think about it, it wasn't such a daft idea. No one other than myself would look into the aircraft – at least, not in the early hours of the morning, and it was generally known that I was going to a wedding in Norwich that morning. There would be no problem in leaving half an hour or so earlier than planned. The only complication, as it turned out, was that you disturbed me while I was dragging the body down the passage. I had no alternative but to leave it there with the suicide note.'

'You saw me put the body under the stairs,' I said. 'Later you removed it when I returned to my room, and you cut the telephone wires. There's only one thing I don't really understand. Why on earth would Lucy want to pin the murder on you?'

'God knows. I told you she is mad.'

'Not too mad to throw the blame on the one apparently stable factor in her life to save herself.'

Suddenly he sagged and looked very tired. 'OK,' he said. 'I've done my best. I'm ready to go now; you can take me to the police station. It's better, anyway, that they should think I did it. If you don't believe my story, I doubt whether anyone else would. As a matter of fact, it really doesn't matter very much any more.'

'Do I count at all in all this?' I asked.

He looked straight at me. I doubt whether he could see me clearly; his eyes were too full of tears.

CHAPTER TWENTY-THREE

After leaving Michael, I drove straight to a flat in Marsham Court in Westminster. I pressed the bell. Bobby Longfellow opened the door to me. It was as if he was expecting me.

The flat, I remember, was in almost total darkness. For some reason, he had not turned the lights on. His round frame was silhouetted against the half light of a window at the end of a passage.

'Ah, Jane,' he said as if he were speaking from a long way away. 'Come in and have a drink.'

'I think the time may have come for you to stop drinking, perhaps for a long while,' I said. 'Can we turn the lights on? It's so dark in here. Do you always sit in darkness, Bobby?'

'When I'm thinking.' He switched on a light in the passage. I followed him into a room on the right, noticing that he was wearing the same olive green shirt that he had had on that morning.

'What is there between you and Lucy?' I asked.

I saw that his double chin had started to shake. 'I just love her, that's all.'

'How much do you love her?'

'I haven't screwed her, if that's what you're getting at, dear girl.'

'Love her enough to convince her to frame Michael.'

He paused and looked at me through half closed

eyes; then he said, 'If you say so. Michael's not everybody's cup of tea, you know; bit of an acquired taste for some people.'

His eyes seemed to close completely and he was pouting his lips. I sensed he was becoming very angry. There was no way I was going to hold back now. I knew that I had the initiative and I was going to keep it that way.

'What you have done is very wicked, Bobby. You must know that it could land you in prison for a very long time.'

Now it was not just his face that was shaking; he was wobbling all over. It was as if at my mention of prison, an electric shock had been passed through his normally sluggish body. The effect was instant; now I sensed it was fear rather than rage which was making him convulse. The man was terrified of going to prison. I increased the pressure on him.

'You even managed to contrive to deceive your friends by pretending to them that you believed John was still alive. It helped, of course, that your chums are a pretty gullible lot; not very admirable types at all really, are they? Not people I would go into the jungle with, anyway.'

'Stop it!' he shouted. 'This is a bad dream. I have always had terrible nightmares, ever since I was a child. In a minute I shall wake up, probably shouting my head off, and it'll all be over.'

He sounded in a panic, but I distrusted him. I felt it was an act. As if to confirm my suspicions, he began to back towards a large mahogany antique bureau. He put his hands behind him. Then I saw him grasp from the top of the desk what looked like a long sharp brass paper knife. I tensed myself for his attack.

'I should put that thing down, if I were you, Bobby. I'm probably stronger than you, certainly in better shape, and you haven't got your girls to protect you.'

He was sweating. I could see he was in a funk. His shirt tails were hanging out of the back of his trousers.

'Go away,' he said. 'Do you hear me? Go away.'

'Let's talk a bit first,' I said. 'Maybe we can do a deal after all.'

'Deal?' he questioned. A new cunning returning to his eyes. He dropped the knife on the floor with a clatter. 'What have you got to offer?'

'I tell you what,' I said. 'I will have that drink after all. I think I've earned it today. Most of it has been unpaid work too. What were you offering me, champagne?'

'If that's what you want.' He was on more familiar territory now. 'I'll go and fetch a bottle from the fridge.' He limped out of the room. I assumed his gout must be hurting him. He turned left in the passage towards the front door. I caught up with him as he wrestled with the latch. I kicked him in his kidneys, hard enough to hurt but not to cause him serious damage; simultaneously I grabbed his wrists. I gave a severe twist to the right one and he let go of the latch. Then I pulled both his arms behind his back and locked them together. He began to scream.

'Champagne, please, Bobby. I think it's the other way.'

'For God's sake, let me go,' he pleaded. 'I won't try anything else.'

I accompanied him to the kitchen and watched him carefully while he pulled out a drawer in the dresser. I could feel myself tense beside him while he searched for what was evidently a rather small object. Then he extracted a pair of round steel-rimmed spectacles. He fixed these to his face and went over to the fridge from where he took out a champagne bottle.

'Moët Chandon, I hope,' I said. I perched on the edge of his kitchen table and sat smiling and dangling my legs.

'So it is true that you need glasses to read.' I must have been looking pretty good, sitting there at ease, and Bobby must have felt pretty humiliated by the whole situation. For the first time for some days I was quite enjoying myself.

'Where shall we talk?' I asked.

'Wherever you bloody well want,' he growled.

'I suppose here will do as well as anywhere,' I said. It meant he would have to stand while I continued to perch on the table in the middle of the room.

'Now,' I said. 'This is the deal. If you don't like it, think about the alternatives.'

'You will admit to having covered up for poor little mad Lucy. I will forget the night you had me abducted at Greysham. I will also do my best to see that life is not made too difficult for you over the missile business.'

'Will I go to prison?' he asked. 'I couldn't bear that.' His face and neck had developed large red blotches.

'Difficult to say. If you confess now, a judge might let you off quite leniently. After all, so far you haven't actually harmed anyone.'

'Done,' he said. 'I'll do it.'

I knew then for certain and for the first time that Michael was innocent of his brother's murder.

EPILOGUE

Following the report of these events which both I and the police made to the Director of Public Prosecutions, it was decided that Antonio's remains should be exhumed. Another autopsy confirmed that the cause of death had been a fall from a polo pony following a heavy intake of heroin and alcohol. There was therefore no reason for the Coroner to re-open the case; the open verdict given by his court has been allowed to stand.

My own view about John Hildreth's role in the affair is that he did believe himself at one time to be responsible for Antonio's death. John did know about the Argentinian's drug addiction and probably knew that he had taken a heavy intake on the day that Antonio played for his polo team. The only questions that can now remain matters for speculation are whether John could have prevented him from playing, whether he appreciated the risk that Antonio was running, whether he cared one way or the other about this risk, and whether or not in the end John actually wished Antonio to injure himself fatally. What is clear is that after the event John was at first filled with some kind of remorse but later began to blame Antonio's death on others.

As for the rest of this tragic party – Lucy Hildreth pleaded guilty to manslaughter with diminished responsibility and the court accepted her plea of insanity; she is now in a hospital for the criminally insane. I went to see her recently; she looks very frail and I cannot believe she will live to a very old age. Perhaps there will be advances in medicine that will bring about some sort of recovery in her mental health.

Bobby Longfellow and Michael Hildreth appeared at the Old Bailey in what were two very notorious trials. The prosecution wanted them both to be convicted of being accessories to murder. In each case, the court found them guilty of conspiring to pervert the course of justice but with extenuating circumstances. They were each given two years' gaol sentences, suspended. Bobby, in particular, did not come over well in court. 'Mercurial' would be the kindest way of describing his performance; on two occasions he was rude beyond belief to the prosecuting council, who the second time retaliated by reducing him to tears. Bobby did not get a good press and subsequently applied for the Chiltern Hundreds, which means he resigned his seat in Parliament.

It's difficult for me to speak objectively about Michael. The newspapers by and large were very sympathetic towards him; they seemed, in particular, to accept that he was driven to do what he did out of love for Lucy. I am sure it comes as no surprise that I also fervently believe this to have been the case. In support of this view, I claim not only what Michael himself has told me, but also what I heard from Leyland before he died of a heart attack in Wormwood Scrubs while he was awaiting his trial for helping to protect Lucy.

I still see quite a lot of Michael, though our relationship is not the easiest of ones. This is partly because we both understand the significance of the fact that he is still married to Lucy (there is no question of his wanting to divorce her). It is also because, perhaps in reaction to this, I have allowed myself to become extremely busy. I am certainly not short of excitement in my life. One day I may come to write up those of my escapades that are no longer subject to the Official Secrets Act. Many of them have involved me in far greater physical danger than the events I have just described. None of them, however, have left me so emotionally exhausted.